SIMPLE DEEDS

SIMPLE DEEDS

A COLLECTION OF URBAN FANTASY SHORT STORIES

HUNTER BLAIN

DEVIN HANSON

JUSTIN LESLIE

CT PHIPPS

Paperback ISBN 978-1-7331873-8-1
eBook ISBN 978-1-7331873-9-8

Contact information for publications
Hunter Blain: info@hunterblain.com
Devin Hanson: author@devinhanson.com
Justin Leslie: Abaddonbooks@hotmail.com
Charles Phipps: charlie_the_cat_pooka@yahoo.com

Contents

PROLOGUE

THROUGHOUT TIME AND space, stars align, wars are fought, and in some cases, paths are crossed. A dropped coin is picked up by another, neither person knowing its fate; a driver swerves, not paying attention, causing the course of others' lives to change; and in some cases, a game is played.

There are many stories and paths that our own fate oftentimes crosses. One entity or action without any seeming connection can touch people not only in our worlds but those of others.

This collection of short stories is one such instance. The characters in this collection, while all living in their own worlds, are somehow touched by an entity sharing the same purpose. To get a simple deed done. Or, is it that simple?

THE HAPPY-TIME HITLER HUNT

A SHORT STORY IN THE PRETERNATURAL CHRONICLES

HUNTER BLAIN

Story takes place alongside book 1, *I'm Glad You're Dead*

CHAPTER 1

"ARE WE THERE yet?" I whined in my transatlantic accent as I rested my cheek on my fist. Staring at the scene outside the transport truck's side window, I noticed the flowers beginning to bloom.

Depweg ignored my question as he drove down the dirt road, apparently making a conscious effort to hit every bump he possibly could.

Shooting a scowl his way, I decided to drop my hand to my lap instead of letting the road continue to pummel my face with my own fist. I swear I could see Depweg stifling a smile.

We had been together since winter, having first teamed up due to our affinity for Nazi slaying, and were slowly making our way to the German stronghold of Berlin in a closing circle. I took pride in knowing we had saved countless innocents while simultaneously taking guiltless pleasure in murdering scores of enemy soldiers set on taking over the world.

My driving force was to spare as many families as I could the pain I had experienced so long ago in Ireland, where my parents had been murdered for their land. I had eluded my fate by allowing my maker to give me my dark gift, but that was a story for another time.

Depweg was wearing a low-level soldier's uniform while I, already having donned my new favorite trench coat that I had taken off of an officer, was dressed as his superior. I was not jiving with the black leather boots that hugged my supermuscular—and not at all fat—calves.

"How many do you think we've stopped?" I asked, my head bobbing slightly with the road.

Depweg shrugged. "Couldn't say. But not enough."

"On that we agree, Mr. Wolf."

"I'm not too keen on that nickname."

"Oh, don't be a fuddy-duddy. It's simple and to the point."

In the distance appeared the unmistakable signs of a roadblock, effectively halting our banter midstride.

"Remember what I said about your German being too perfect," Depweg reminded me as he began shifting the gears down and slowing our momentum.

"Yeah, yeah," I said in less-than-perfect German. Most supes had the innate ability of mimicking the language around them. I had always figured it was an evolutionary trait that helped us blend in with the mortals. It just so happened my German was a little too on point and drew attention.

We came to a stop and Depweg leaned one of his massive arms on the window while tilting his head closer to acknowledge the guard.

In a natural German accent, as my friend had been born in the country, Depweg greeted, "Empty transport heading back to base for maintenance."

The soldier stepped up on the foothold of the truck, peered into the cab at me, and scanned my outfit.

"Can I assist you with something, soldier?" I aggressively asked with the air of authority one would expect from a commanding officer. I tried to bathe my purple eyes in the shadow cast by the brim of my officer's hat.

"*Gefreiter*, actually," he retorted, giving me a feeling of unease and annoyance. Unease, not because I thought he might be able to harm me in any way but because the jig was up, and I might have failed in my performance.

The corporal continued, "Why is a *Generalmajor* overseeing a standard maintenance run?"

"I don't see how that's any of your business, *Gefreiter*," I put emphasis on his title, warning him of his transgres—

Machine-gun fire erupted from the corporal's MG 42 machine gun, punching holes in the thin metal of the driver's side door and my new werewolf friend, who was still in his man-suit.

Depweg lashed out with a preternaturally powerful arm and backhanded the corporal in the face, effectively removing his lower jaw with a sickening crunch and a tearing sound.

Depweg lifted his other hand from his side, now coated in fresh blood.

"Ow," he grunted between clenched teeth.

Soldiers began pouring into view from all directions, springing the trap they had set, their automatic rifles pointing in our direction before burping round after round into the cabin.

Depweg dropped down onto the bench seat, covering his head with his thick arms while I flung myself on top of him, protecting his vital organs the best I could with my impervious body.

My werewolf friend let out a guttural scream as a barrage of bullets found a place to retire inside his exposed flank. The smell of copious amounts of blood wafted into my nose, instantly making my mouth salivate while also bringing a feeling of guilt that it was my friend's wounds from which the aroma arose. I could feel my large friend shuddering with each impact as if being struck with electricity.

After several seconds, the firing ceased, and I could make out a few tentative footsteps as two soldiers approached both sides of the cabin.

"Play dead. That's a good boy," I whispered to my were friend, who grunted once in confirmation. I was confident only his backside and legs had taken any real damage, and he would heal those wounds with a quick snack of filet mig-Nazi.

While closing my eyes to play the part of a corpse, I sent out my other senses and heard the two blood bags climbing up to peer into the truck that now resembled Swiss cheese.

"I think we got them!" the soldier hanging on my side of the truck called out to his comrades.

Being a vampire afforded me with some—shall we say, fun—abilities. One of which was the control over my preternatural energy in the form of blood manifestations. Anything my mind could imagine, I could create, within the parameter that there were no chemical components needed. For example, I could will melee weapons like swords, knives, hammers, and the like, but I couldn't create guns that required an explosive chemical to fire the projectile.

Blurring into a seated position, I willed a rod comprised of my blood to shoot from my palm and down the soldier's gaping, surprised mouth, stopping once I reached his juicy center.

"Think again," I corrected as I let my fangs elongate and eyes turn from the purple of sunset to the crimson of predation and terror.

I willed my manifestation to shoot out spikes in all directions, piercing every major organ in the soldier's writhing torso and drawing his blood into myself. His life energy flowed into my construct before becoming one with my own, adding to my well of ancient power.

The soldier tried to scream, which contracted his throat and pushed my bloodspikes deeper into his supple flesh, which, ironically, caused him to shriek with renewed gusto.

Magazines were ejected while trembling hands fumbled with spares all around the half circle of men standing just outside the front of the truck.

I stood up on the bench seat, tearing a hole through the thin metal cabin as if it were nothing more than aluminum foil, and stared with fierce eyes at the soon-to-be-dead fools that dared to fire upon me.

With a quick flick of my arm and retraction of my manifestation, I threw the lifeless, pale corpse toward one of his buddies, who had been the closest to being able to fire his weapon again. He tumbled backward with bone-shattering force while a grunt of air blasted from his collapsing lungs, which were being shredded by jagged, broken ribs.

Hearing the unmistakable sound of a round being chambered, I cartwheeled sideways over the hood of the truck, intentionally drawing fire away from my wounded were friend. In his man-suit, he was susceptible to firearms, silver or not.

A staccato of panicked automatic fire, accompanied by a strobe light of flashes, filled the night. Some of the men even screamed with wide-eyed terror, which was odd to me. I didn't think they had had enough time to process what was happening and understand that I wasn't a mortal. That suggested they knew we were coming.

A round struck my back, mushrooming harmlessly off my all-but-impervious skin. Then a thought came to mind that a hole had probably just been punched in my new favorite coat.

"Lilith damn it!" I cried out, knowing I'd have to be careful if I wanted it to survive the ambush. Or I could just remove it, I suppose, though that would be admitting to myself that I couldn't handle the humans as efficiently as I thought I could. I did think quite a lot of myself, and for just reasons. Eh, time to start cooking with gas.

I crouched down while pivoting before shooting out with powerful legs like a spear toward the mortal who was having trouble controlling his recoil. I brought my forearms up and crossed them over my face, willing impossibly sharp bloodblades down their lengths as I flew.

As I smashed into the soldier, I shot my arms out in either direction and cut the man in half at the waist before passing through the widening space between torso and legs.

I quickly tucked in midair and landed on my feet as I turned to catch the two pieces of the man.

"Want to see a magic trick?" I asked the remaining soldiers, who were paralyzed with a fear that they had never thought fathomable in their entire lives.

I began siphoning the spilling blood from the two halves, willing them to fly through the air and into my open mouth in thick, crimson streams that defied gravity. It was euphoric, and I had to force myself to keep my eyes open lest I risk my coat attempting to match the cabin of the truck.

"Vampir!" one of the men cried out as he dropped his gun and sprinted into the darkness of the surrounding woods.

I willed a blooddagger with a rope attached, and was about to throw it at the fleeing man when a white sheet of pain exploded up my leg, stealing my breath in a yelp of agony. A boom barked out a split second later.

I collapsed to the knee that wasn't screaming out and looked down to see my other had exploded. Blood flowed freely from the dangling flesh that hung outside of my shredded pant leg like freshly ground beef dropping from a meat grinder.

There was a popping sound from somewhere that could have been miles away in my staggered state. I thought I heard a man grunting so low that only my ears could pick it up. My eyes flicked to the truck cabin for a moment before shooting back to the ground.

Drool spilled over a quivering lip as I looked up with a shaky head to see a Nazi officer holding a Luger P08 with a smoking barrel. He had been waiting in the guard shack for his moment to strike. I was also vaguely aware of the unmistakable sound of some sort of small motor starting up somewhere in the distance.

With the blooddagger remaining in the grip of my right hand, trembling hands tried to wrap around the loose flesh of my knee as I desperately tried to will the gaping wound closed. It refused my command, and all I could do was stare at the barrel of his weapon in utter disbelief.

"Silver rounds," the officer said with the wry smile of a predator that had caught his prey. I did not enjoy the sudden reversal of the food chain. Not one bit. "You were careless and left a clear trail. It took us a few months, but we finally found you, Vampir."

"Let me guess, you plan on letting me go so I don't kill you, am I right? I am open to hearing you beg if you are comfortable dropping to your knees in front of your men."

The officer pshawed while shaking his head in disappointment, never letting his gun waver.

"We are going to cut you open and find out what makes you tick, abomination."

I pivoted and began pushing off with my good leg in an effort to attack when my other knee exploded, dropping me to the ground with a shriek I couldn't hold in.

"Tsk, tsk, tsk," the officer breathed out as he took a few steps toward me, pulling a tight rope made of silver from his pocket. The pistol that was still trained on me wafted white smoke from the barrel.

My eyes went wide as I understood that he meant what he had said. They were going to cut me open, probably with silver or iron tools, and poke around inside me. I felt a fear, then, I hadn't felt since my days as a fledgling vampire. Ulric had been a harsh teacher.

"Your essence will be used to enhance our elite soldiers, setting the stage to overthrow the entire world under the flag of the Third Reich."

There was a grunt coming from the cabin of the truck, prompting the hunter to take notice and glance around.

"Only one problem with that, you Nazi shithead," I growled between clenched teeth. "You won't be alive much longer to take me in."

"How many were in the truck?" the hunter asked hurriedly over his shoulder.

"T-two, sir," one of the men answered shakily.

"Fool! Why didn't you tell m—" the hunter began before an eight-foot-long, five-hundred-pound werewolf burst through the top of the truck's cabin, tearing it apart as if it had been made from sheets of paper.

The muzzle of the Luger began swiping the air to point at the wolf when the blooddagger I had been holding rocketed from my grasp as I moved my arm at impossible speeds.

The dagger shattered the pistol right as the trigger was squeezed, sending a round flying randomly into the night.

"ARGH!" the hunter cried out as he clutched at his bleeding hand. "Bastard!"

The wolf landed on one of the stunned soldiers, removing his throat in a swift motion before charging the next closest.

Rampant gunfire sounded as the enormous yet nimble wolf pounced on his targets, removing limbs or throats without resistance like swatting at a fresh mound of fluffy snow.

With incredible speed, I crawled on my hands to the nearest soldier, who was focused on the brown wolf that was now glistening in the moonlight with fresh blood, as if coated in reflective rubies.

I willed spikes into my hands and plunged the first into the ample meat of the soldier's thigh, siphoning blood as I moved, and climbed up to sink the other into his pelvis. With a hold on his leg and torso, I moved my fangs up to the soldier's neck and bit in with enough force that I tore tendons, and even scraped his vertebrae.

With violent intensity, I inhaled the mortal's entire supply of blood in mere moments; quick enough that he didn't even drop to the ground until after the last drop had been claimed. His heart continued to pound erratically, not knowing the battle was over even as his eyes went glassy and unfocused.

With the stolen energy, I quickly sat up and willed my spikes to form hollow cylinders, took a deep breath, and slammed them into the holes on my knees, effectively removing the tissue that had been struck by the silver.

Once removed, I was able to close my wounds with ease. Sons of bitches knew to coat the rounds in some sort of residue to prevent healing.

Shooting to my feet on my repaired legs, I focused on the next closest soldier, who was trying to slap in a fresh magazine, and blurred to him faster than any mortal eye could see.

Reaching my next meal, I lifted him by his throat and was about to will bloodclaws to pierce his flesh and exsanguinate the precious blood within when a silver rod lodged into my wrist.

With a bark of electrified pain, I dropped the soldier while slowly bringing my wrist up to inspect the damage. A heavy rod with a sharp, crimson-coated tip sticking through my arm seemed to wave at me in greeting.

With gritted teeth, I slowly pivoted my head to regard the hunter, who was pulling another rod from the inside of a trench coat that almost exactly matched my own.

"Hey! I don't have loop thingies," I cried out while pointing my numb hand his way. "Oh . . . right," I whispered to myself while trying to wiggle my lifeless fingers. Only my pinky was fully functioning, with my ring finger trying its best to follow suit.

With a grunt, I yanked the rod free right as the hunter threw another one my way. Without even having to think, I threw my own to intercept the Nazi's. They clanged in midair, with my rod winning the game of inertia and smacking his backward to disappear into the woods, tumbling in the darkness with mine close behind.

The soldier who I had dropped by my feet had apparently caught his breath and was trying to scramble away. Without taking my eyes off the hunter, I slammed a bloodspear into the liver of the soldier and sucked all the life essence from his blood-soaked organ. It was delectable, and it made my skin bubble with goose bumps as a shudder went up my spine.

After the human was reduced to a shriveled, pale husk with a gaping mouth perpetually locked in horror, I yanked the spear free before twirling it in a dramatic show for the hunter.

He pulled out two more silver spikes and held them in either hand, spinning them to match my flair. His face was determined, but with a glistening brow. I could see the arteries in his neck pounding against the skin, showcasing his controlled fear.

I smiled at him and bellowed my challenge, prompting the hunter to return his own roar, right as a five-hundred-pound mass of muscles, fangs, and claws smashed into the mortal man. His torso was shoved to the side, moving faster than his head and legs, and the limbs that were too slow to catch up were broken at the connecting points.

Joints were snapped at the hips, while the vertebrae in the neck shattered into fragments resembling broken glass dropped from the top of a tall building. I watched in fascination as an ear smashed into his shoulder before his skull rebounded and the other side followed suit, like a ringing bell in a church tower.

My eyes were locked on his, and I watched as his gaze went from fierce and focused to glazed and empty in a fraction of a second. His face didn't contort into the painful scowl that one might expect. He simply . . . died.

Depweg landed on top of him, his dripping fangs already tearing into the flesh of the hunter with intense vigor.

I cringed into an O face as his massive jaws latched onto an arm and shook it violently with his muscular neck, rending the arm free with a delicious tearing sound. I didn't know if it was from the leather coat or the muscle and other connective tissue. Probably both.

Glancing around, I saw horrifically mangled corpses that were missing entire limbs, throats, and even entrails.

"Golly gee, Mr. Wolf. Did you save any for your old pal?" I asked as Depweg finished crunching the rest of the arm before swallowing, bone and all. Fingers slid down his throat and almost seemed to wave me a final farewell. I might have gulped.

Glistening, matted fur at his hindquarters caught my eye, and I saw where the initial barrage of bullets had impacted him. I guessed they would be healing now that he had consumed several pounds of man meat. And when I said several, I, of course, meant around a hundred. Oops, wait a sec, he was eating the hunter. All of him.

I tugged at my collar with my index finger as I turned from the carnage. Now, I wouldn't describe myself as having a weak stomach, but watching an entire human being get eaten by a voracious wolf was enough to make my throat warn me of my stomach's intentions of purging its contents. It's just something I had never borne witness to before.

Curiosity got the better of me as I briefly wondered how he would consume the pelvis with all that bone. I dared a glance and realized something; curiosity could go to hell.

"Oh my Lilith," I exhaled as I turned back and hunched over, grabbing my knees. I began spitting intermittently, trying to keep the vomit down. "Don't . . . don't do it," I commanded my stomach.

A resounding crunch smashed into my ears, and my brain filled in the picture of what was happening behind me with exaggerated detail.

"Oh nooOOOOOOO," I cried out as my stomach won the revolt and spewed the blood I had swallowed. At least I had already absorbed the energy.

Once my completely voluntary task of vomiting was over, I looked up to see the place where the hunter had been hiding from view.

After a surprisingly short few minutes, Depweg padded over to the guard shack I had started inspecting, chuffing once to signal he was done with his snack. He was still licking the abundant gore from his muzzle.

Dropping the useless documents I was scanning, I looked at him with an arched eyebrow and asked, "Where does all that meat go, Mr. Wolf? You literally ate his clothes too."

Depweg turned his head to regard his flank. I followed his gaze and saw that the oozing bullet wounds had stopped bleeding and were slowly cinching closed. His healing wasn't anywhere near as fast as mine, but it was still damn impressive.

"I think the coast is clear if you would like to put your man-suit back on."

Depweg chuffed once before stepping outside the shack and beginning the change.

"Though I don't know where you'll find any clothes," I said just above a whisper as I looked out at the clearing of carelessly consumed corpses copiously coated in crimson. "Oh, and we will need to make this look like an ambush from the Allies."

As Depweg's tendons popped, fur was replaced by skin, and fangs fell out to be replaced by human teeth, I gathered the bodies littering the ground and threw them in the back of the transport truck with ease.

After the last of the Nazis had been tossed in the back and Depweg had stolen bits of unsoiled clothing from different soldiers, he asked, "Now what?" as he regarded the truck.

"I want to try something I've been working on," I admitted as I clapped my hands and began rubbing my palms together. "Stand back."

Depweg looked at me, shrugged, and turned to walk to the edge of the clearing, staring off into the woods as he did. It was as if something was bothering him.

I concentrated on the exposed gas tank of the transport truck and focused on exciting the molecules of the metal. I had had a moderate amount of success in lighting small fires in gas lamps and torches, but hadn't tried anything of this siz—

The gas tank exploded without preamble, sending me flying backward as a fireball shot into the sky. I landed on my ass and tumbled end over end, coming to a stop some twenty feet away on my ample rear.

With my legs out in front of me and my hands resting limply on my now dusty thighs, I stared with wide eyes while blowing my long black hair out of my face.

"Neat!"

"Way to go, fathead," Depweg chided as he strolled over to where I sat, giving the flaming truck a wide berth. He stuck out his hand and I grabbed it, pulling myself to a standing position.

Pulling my gaze from the inferno, I gave my were friend a once over and saw that his shirt was a full size too small.

"Couldn't find anything smaller?" I jested.

"This was the only one without blood all over it."

The thought of a uniform without blood sparked a pile of gunpowder in my head.

"One got away!" I cried out, palming my forehead. "He yelled, 'Vampir,' and then disappeared into the woods."

"Which way did he go?" Depweg asked, immediately scanning the surrounding area.

"Um, I think that way," I pointed, unsure.

"You think?" Depweg asked, crossing his arms as he turned to face me.

"You see, Mr. Wolf, I had just been shot in the knee with a silver round and my attention was elsewhere. You know how it goes." I bent slightly while keeping my eyes on my friend and patted the bare skin of my knees to emphasize my point.

"He couldn't have gotten far," Depweg mused to himself as he turned back to the woods and began walking around the perimeter, presumably searching for signs of the missing Nazi. It had been my experience that Depweg could track prey with the best of them.

"We are close enough to our goal that I suggest we press forward," I recommended as I patted the dirt from what remained of my pants and my sturdy coat. My pant legs below the knee were around my ankles, and I reached down to rip them off, effectively creating shorts. "Well, this doesn't look odd at all," I whispered to myself as I shifted my weight and turned one shiny boot back and forth in the dim light of the shack before switching to the other.

"You might be right."

"Which part? Pressing forward or how odd I look?"

"Both."

I placed my hands on my hips and looked around as I strolled down the road in the direction we had been heading before the roadblock had stopped us. Depweg took my cue and followed suit.

It didn't take long to locate what I was looking for.

"Here's one," I said, jogging up to the sleek, black Mercedes that was hidden behind some trees just off the road. "Oh my! It appears that our hunter friend was some sort of high-ranking official. Neat!"

I climbed into the passenger seat of the long convertible car with two bench seats covered in nice leather. Depweg jumped into the driver's side and started the ignition, which thundered to life with a satisfying rumble that lightly vibrated my entire body.

"Say what you want about the Nazis, they make some neat vehicles."

"The Nazis didn't make it, John. Germans did. Not every German is a damn Nazi," Depweg corrected aggressively as he turned a stern gaze to lock onto me.

Throwing my hands up in placation, I said, "Duly noted."

He stared at me a moment longer before turning to face forward and pulling onto the dirt road. The long car surprisingly had decent shocks as we traveled at a moderate speed toward our intended target. My hands ran across the plush leather of the interior while my hair blew forward, for some reason.

"What the . . ." I drawled as I tried brushing my hair behind my ears. Apparently, I had lost my fancy officer hat at some point and now my shoulder-length black hair was warring with my face.

We made it the rest of the way to the outskirts of Berlin without molestation, giving me time to explore the contents of the Mercedes, which had accumulated a thin layer of dirt on its glossy exterior.

While searching, I found a Walther PPK in the glove box.

"Hello," I exulted. "What's this?" I picked up the weapon and searched for a way to check the ammunition. When I didn't see one, I brought up the barrel and tried to look down its length.

"What are you doing?" Depweg asked, gently yet firmly pushing the weapon's muzzle away from my face.

"Trying to see what the bullets are."

Depweg held out his hand, palm up, and I placed the pistol in his grip. Bringing the gun to his nose, he sniffed a few times before handing it back to me and saying, "Not silver."

"Eh, I still want it," I admitted, pocketing the Walther in my breast pocket. "A keepsake."

After a few minutes of driving around a surprisingly silent edge of town, we stopped at another barricade that led to the heart of Berlin.

Hard faces stared at us, making me uncomfortable. Had I mentioned that I did not like the predator-to-prey role reversal?

Off to the side sat a motorcycle that was still popping from being recently driven. I scowled as my brain tried to connect the dots between two stubborn points that repelled one another like magnets. A thin layer of dust coating the bike waved a warning flag.

The two dots connected with electrified urgency as I realized I had heard a motor start after the soldier who had cried out "Vampir" had fled. The dirt matched that of our car.

"Oh . . . fuck . . ." I drawled, drawing Depweg's attention from the stern eyes that stared at us.

In slow motion, he began turning toward what I was looking at right as some movement caught my eye. I shifted my focus to witness the same soldier I had seen fleeing into the woods come around a corner with a horrifying man made out of metal. Of course, he wasn't actually made of metal, simply covered from head to toe, with articulated joints and slits for his eyes. It was what was in his hands that made a tiny bit of pee escape my Little John.

A long canister with a pistol grip rested in the metal man's hands, a small flame hissing at the end. A thick hose at the grip connected to a huge backpack with two more canisters that contained some sort of liquid.

Depweg saw my eyebrows shoot for the safety of my hairline and turned to witness two more metal soldiers come into view with identical canister weapons in hand.

"Oh . . . fuck . . ." Depweg agreed.

"It's them!" the coward soldier cried out while frantically pointing at us.

I lifted a finger to my chest and asked, "Me?" right as a torrent of flames spewed from the lead metal man's weapon.

The fire flowed like water, coating the entire front of the vehicle in hungry flames. The attack splashed over the windshield and into the back seat, catching the leather on fire as if it had been soaked in fuel.

"OH LILITH!" I shrieked as my brain panicked on what to do, like a golden retriever in a field of never-ending tennis balls.

I lowered myself to the floorboard while Depweg crouched and slammed on the gas with the Mercedes in first gear. I could feel the beast of a vehicle rocketing forward, accompanied by a shrill scream of surprise that was followed closely by a thump and the feeling of slamming into something. We bounced once, hard, as something large lodged under the carriage before an explosion spewed flames in all directions from beneath the car.

"JESUS!" Depweg roared as shrieks of unimaginable agony stemmed from the soldiers that had surrounded the vehicle, now dressed head to toe in ravenous flames. It was a good look for them.

"HOLD ON!" I yelled as I grabbed Depweg's wrist and leaped into the air. At least, I tried to. My feet went through the floorboard to strike the concrete some ten inches below, which effectively diminished my potential momentum to a catastrophic level.

Instead of flying into the air above the rooftops to land safely away from the raging fire, we jumped around twelve feet straight up, our momentum coming to a halt with alarming quickness.

As we began to fall back toward the inferno, I spun in midair and tossed the heavy Depweg into the street several yards behind the Mercedes. I felt his wrist pop from the sudden and extreme force. To his credit, he didn't cry out.

"RRRAAAAH!" he bellowed a split second later—so never mind about that credit.

The car rushed up to catch me like a catcher's mitt that was also on fire. The flames seemed to beckon like sultry fingers, urging me to let them embrace my handsome body.

I tucked into my leather trench coat as best as I could while definitely not shrieking in a pitch reserved for a teapot coming to a boil.

Because my luck was always in—and always bad—I landed in the oh-so-comfortable back seat that was almost entirely comprised of harmless flames. Did I say harmless? Because I meant harmful. Much harm. Ample harm, even.

My hair went up in a smoking puff as I scrambled to urgently remove myself from the Mer-flame-ies while desperately trying to keep my skin from conflagrating. Credit to my trench coat for keeping the flames at bay.

That's when the fuel tank decided to join the fray and ignite.

As I tumbled over the side, the car exploded, throwing me into a nearby building with a delicate, almost pleasant, whack of leather on brick.

"Ow. Ow, ow. Ow," I wheezed out as I fell on top of my head and dropped to my side before pushing myself up into a seated position. White/gray smoke wafted up my face from where my beard had just been. "Ah man, not my beard."

"John!" I heard Depweg yelling from somewhere nearby.

Pivoting my head, which seemed to weigh a hundred pounds right then, I saw my new friend running toward me. He was grasping the wrist I had broken, and he yanked it back into place with a grunt.

Without another word, he grabbed my collar with his good hand, lifted me over his massive shoulder, and sprinted further into the city.

"WATCH OUT!" I screamed while pointing in the direction of the two surviving metal men who creepily walked through the flames and were orienting on us. Of course, Depweg probably couldn't see where I was pointing with my torso behind his back.

They shot a torrent of flames in front of our path in anticipation of our movement. Depweg was running too fast to stop before we entered the flame geysers.

Reacting on instinct, I lashed out with my left hand and shot fingers that were electrified with urgency into the brick wall we were running next to. I stiffened my legs where I was bent over his shoulder and tried to push up with my knees, arresting our momentum while Depweg let out an, "Oomph," as air rocketed from his lungs.

My fingers created ditches in the brick wall, giving me a moment of panic at the thought that I wouldn't be able to stop us. Then they stopped, and Depweg's feet went out from under him, his toes getting splashed with the liquid fire of the metal men.

Using the wall as leverage, I pulled my stomach in like I was doing an abdominal crunch while pulling with my left hand, and threw us several feet backward.

We tumbled for a few rolls before I came up on my feet. I saw Depweg patting at his with his good hand, extinguishing the flames eating at them.

The metal men turned to face us with their expressionless helmets, and pointed their flamethrowers.

I felt something in my left hand and understood without having to look that I was holding a portion of the brick wall.

I stepped forward with my right foot and threw the chunk of brick at the first metal man with all my might. Unfortunately for me, I was right-handed, and the brick went wide and smacked into a wall that was nowhere near the men.

The two metal dickheads looked down at themselves before switching to lock gazes with one another. After a moment, they began laughing with muffled voices before turning the slits of their eyes toward me, ready to finish the job.

With preternatural speed that was fueled by embarrassed rage, I slashed at the wall next to me with my right hand and threw the crumbling rocks in an arc toward the men.

The first was riddled with dents as several small fragments tried, and failed, to pierce the metal of the suit.

The second fire-Nazi had one of the massive tanks on his back rupture at the nozzle. He dropped his weapon and began waving his arms behind him while shrieking with the delicious panic of helplessness.

The first, instead of helping his comrade, understood the futility of the situation and began taking quick side steps away from the soon-to-be dead man.

The second metal man's tank began belching out flames for a few short seconds until both tanks exploded in a satisfying ball of fire. The shrieks went out immediately. Whether this was from all the oxygen being consumed in an instant, his vocal cords melting, or a combination of the two, I didn't know.

The first—and now only—metal man spewed a torrent of raging fire in my direction as I marveled at the sheer amount of light being projected in the area.

Depweg slammed into me, throwing me out of the way of the fire as the voracious flame smashed into the building I had been standing next to. The night became as bright as day from the light of the raging fires.

Letting my body once again operate purely on instinct, I willed a bloodrope to shoot out of my palm and lashed it at the metal man's feet. It wrapped around both ankles, and I yanked with my incredible strength, causing the heavy man to fall backward while his finger still squeezed the trigger of the hazardous weapon.

Flames arched into the air until his arm was pointing straight up into the night sky, only for them to reverse direction and begin to fall back onto the man who had begun to scream in understanding of his blunder.

Fire as flowing as water rained onto the metal man, seeking anything flammable to consume.

He let go of the trigger and dropped the weapon, which clattered to the ground next to him as he patted his face with ungraceful metal hands. Understanding dawned as I realized the only portion of the man's body that could be exposed to the flames was the eye slits in the metal helmet.

"Oh, Lilith," I drawled with a cringe as the man screamed with sickening intensity while desperately trying to get at the fire eating at his face inside his helmet. Then I remembered he was a Nazi shithead, and my cringe was replaced with a toothy smile as satisfying flames danced in my eyes.

"We need to go," Depweg urged as he grabbed my arm just above the elbow, drawing my attention from the man who had stopped screaming, though he still tried to get his helmet off with weakening fingers that had begun to slow precipitously. "John, they know we are coming."

Turning to my were friend, I broke myself from the moment, processed what he'd said, then nodded once.

"You're right. Let's move," I agreed as I turned to face the city.

"He's in a bunker not far from here," Depweg informed as he began a light jog.

"How do you know?" I inquired.

"A, ah, man told me."

Now it was my turn to grab my friend's arm, halting his jog.

"What do you mean?" I asked harshly, wanting to know why I was only just now finding out about this crucial bit of information.

Depweg stared at me with eyes that suggested he was expecting this conversation.

"A few months ago, a man approached me during the day while you slept, and told me where we could find Hitler."

"And you are only just now telling me this because . . . ?" I asked with a hand that circled the air, suggesting he finish the thought.

"I guess I forgot."

"Considering that we were almost just incinerated by Nazi shitheads armed with guns that can shoot fire like water, not to mention the trap earlier tonight, can I suggest you not forget anything else pertinent?" I was harsh in my assessment of the situation. "How do we know we aren't walking right into a trap?!"

"He was a German soldier who was rebelling against the Third Reich. Just like me."

"Like you?" I asked, cocking my head.

"I'm German, but know Hitler and his cronies must be stopped at all costs. Not only because what he is doing is wrong but also because I heard the Allies have a massive weapon that could wipe my country off the map."

"Whoa, really?"

"That's just what I heard."

"So what about this soldier?"

"I found him walking away from where we were heading, and he told me he had information that could help us."

"Hold on there a second, Mr. Wolf. You are saying he just offered up information like that? All willy-nilly? Not to give you a bum rap, but that sounds suspicious."

"John, I'm cutting to the chase for the sake of time."

"Well, I'd like to know more about this soldier you happened to run into, if you don't mind."

As we walked at a moderate pace, he explained the story to me.

"I was foraging for food when I heard him walking through the brush. We noticed each other about the same time, and he took off running. I chased him, thinking he was a Nazi off to warn his comrades."

"Alright. I'm with you so far."

"I caught him easily, and he was so terrified I was going to hurt him that it gave me pause because I was wearing an enlisted soldier's uniform. I saw that he had torn all identifying markers off and questioned why. He told me, in a defiant tone, that he wasn't going to do the Reich's bidding anymore, even if it meant his death."

"That's when you told him we were on the same side," I guessed.

"Right. I could sense he was telling the truth and told him that Hitler wouldn't be a problem for much longer. He grew excited and told me he had information that might help. So, of course, I listened."

"I think I see where this is going. Still, I don't like all these traps that have conveniently been set for us."

"The hunter said it himself that we had left a trail he had followed."

"Bah, I suppose you're right. Besides, we are here now. I still don't like it, though."

"At least you got your hair back."

I lifted an arm so my fingers could explore the thick reddish beard and long black hair that had grown back.

"There was also something about him. Something that made me feel . . . well, I don't know what."

"What do you mean?" I asked, turning to regard my friend who was trying to find the right words.

"His eyes, and even his hair, seemed to glow in the sunlight. I-I've never seen eyes like that."

"O . . . kay. So his eyes glowed. How does that help us believe him?"

"I didn't say they glowed. I said they seemed to glow. But, like I said, I could sense the man was telling the truth."

"You can do that? I mean, I can usually read a mortal's heartbeat and shift in their pupils to see if they are lying. It's a trick I picked up on over the years."

"I can smell the change in their skin when someone lies. They usually sweat more when nervous, and my nose catches the change. After he knew we were on the same side, his body didn't change."

I considered what he was saying while chewing on my cheek.

"What do you think?" Depweg asked, throwing me off.

"What do I think? A little late for that, wouldn't you say?" Depweg stared back at me, and I softened my tone. "I don't know, Mr. Wolf. You're the military expert, right?"

"Hmph," Depweg responded, crossing his massive arms over his chest, deep in thought.

"Hmph? 'Hmph' isn't an answer there, my friend."

"I think we are this close and should press on. And stop calling me 'Mr. Wolf.'"

"And if there are more traps?" I asked, placing both hands on my hips while ignoring his request.

"We will adapt to the situations as they arise."

"I don't know about you, Deppyweg, but I sure don't enjoy those flame gun things." Something else came to mind. "Can you shift to your mean face? I'd like to hurry up and get this done, if we can."

"Good idea," Depweg said as he began stripping off his odd-fitting clothing. I noticed his hand was already usable again.

Joints popped as hair began growing over his entire body before thickening into fur. Hands and feet extended while a snout pushed out from his human face. Brown eyes shifted to yellow orbs with black slits running up their middle.

Within a minute or so, an eight-foot wolf—from tip of the nose to base of the tail—stood on all fours. He chuffed once and then shook like a dog out of water before lifting his massive head to sniff the air.

"Are you ready, boy?" I asked playfully.

Depweg locked eerie yellow eyes on me and scowled with an accompanying growl.

"Whoa there, fella. I didn't mean to rub your rhubarb!" I threw out with palms held out placatingly.

Depweg growled again, but with much less gusto.

"Is your, um, wrist better?" I asked, looking at the spot on his long arm I thought could have been his wrist.

In answer, the giant wolf took off in a dead sprint.

"I'll take that as a yes," I whispered to myself as I ran to catch up.

He was fast in his wolf form, and we made excellent time. A few times, Depweg took drastic turns down back alleys in an effort to avoid any more checkpoints, just in case they were expecting us.

We came to the edge of a building that looked fortified, with guards all around. Depweg chuffed and pointed his nose toward the ground.

"Alright, Mr. Wolf. You take the right guards and I'll tak—" I started before Depweg leapt into the fray and began mauling soldiers who didn't even have enough time to gasp in preparation for their final screams.

From the corner of my vision, I saw another group of men start to rouse and bring up their rifles to aim at my wolf buddy while barking out curses in German.

Willing a bloodgladius, I blurred toward them at preter-speed and lobbed off their heads at the shoulders. Bodies went rag doll, no longer receiving signals from the brain, as heads went tumbling like bowling balls. Not able to help myself, I siphoned their spewing blood out of the toppled corpses, trying not to moan as I drank. I lived for the fix and couldn't let fresh blood go to waste.

Once all the soldiers had been taken care of, Depweg sauntered over to where I stood, inspecting the building.

I let my eyes, which were still in predatory mode, scan the building in search of any heat signatures as I wiped any excess blood from my lips.

"Hmm, that's odd," I said to myself. "Must be extrathick walls." I turned to my werewolf friend and said, "Maybe we should try the front door?"

In answer, Depweg turned and began a canter to the large front entrance of the bunker I later learned was called "Führerbunker." I kid you not! If I ever had a bunker, I was now torn between calling it John-Bunker or The Fortress of Solitaire. I admit the later was stolen from a comic that introduced a new superhero in red tights a few years prior. I think his name was Superman or something that would never take off, and had the Fortress of Solitude to call home. But, you know, mine was a play on words with that card game . . . you know what? Never mind.

The doors were barricaded with something on the other side, so I did the obvious thing and punched it. Nothing happened. Well, I said nothing happened, but the bones in my knuckles kind of shattered as the metal rang out in defiance.

"Well, this bunker has moxie if I do say so myself," I admired while rubbing my hand, letting it heal with audible cracks. "What are you willing to bet this goes underground?"

Depweg looked up at me and cocked his head in question as if to ask, "What do you mean?"

"That should be higher up," I pointed at a water tower that was on ground level. "Coincidentally, Mr. Wolf, that is also our way in."

Yellow eyes flicked between the water tower and me a few times before he nodded once in reluctant acceptance.

We padded over to where the large tank sat, and I placed a hand on the thick line that ran underground. It looked big enough for a man to squeeze down, but I doubted anything bigger.

"I don't think you'll be able to fit, Mr. Wolf," I admitted, making a show of eyeing his bulk. He then dropped to all fours and seemed to collapse in on himself; not in a preternatural way or anything, just how dogs and cats always seemed to be able to fit in tight places.

Then he plopped back up after proving his point, looked me in the eyes, and dropped his gaze to my stomach. To emphasize his subtle question, he poked at my belly with his nose.

"Hey now, careful. You'll bust your nose on my rock-solid muscles," I said confidently while pretending to flex. He poked at my stomach again. "Hey, hey! I'll fit. I'll fit! Don't you fret one bit."

Depweg chuffed, but not in agreement. Instead, I got the subtle feeling that it was more in curiosity of the spectacle that he was about to witness.

With a swipe of my hand, I separated the tube as if it were made of twigs, and was rewarded with a blast of water that smashed into Depweg and me.

We tumbled in the resulting tsunami, coming to a stop some thirty or forty feet away.

I lifted one of the wet flaps of my trench off my face while spitting out a mouthful of water like a fancy fountain.

Depweg got to his feet and growled at me before padding closer to where I lay. I lazily turned my head to look at him right as he shook what had to be gallons of water off his thick fur, coating me in a fresh shower.

"Neat. Now I smell like wet dog," I lamented while continuing to lie on my back. Depweg's face shot my way with another growl before something gleamed in his eyes.

He lifted his leg in my general direction and I blurred to my feet in an instant.

"Would you look at the time," I said while lifting my wet cuff to expose my bare wrist. "It's Happy-time Hitler Hunt . . . um . . . ti-time," I finished lamely. Depweg seemed to lower his head in shame at my horrible naming prowess.

We sloshed through the wet grass of the grounds to the hole in the ground that was full of water.

"Hope you can hold your breath a long time," I said while looking at my friend with concern.

He shifted on his feet and whined once in answer.

"I have an idea," I said with an index finger shooting up to point to the sky in victory. "Let me go first. You'll know when to follow."

Depweg nodded in understanding as he plopped down on his behind and began scanning the surrounding area like a sentry.

"GERONIMO!" I yelled as I jumped into the air and pivoted to dive into the pipe headfirst with my hands pointed toward the hole.

I, um, might have missed and landed on solid ground with a grunt while rolling in the wet grass. The stars were above me with wafts of light gray clouds flying overhead. I admired them as I remained on my back, groaning as I stared into the heavens.

There was a staccato of high-pitched whining, and I scowled while turning my head to see a five-hundred-pound wolf covering his muzzle with his paws as he appeared to be fighting with himself not to make noise.

"Are . . . are you laughing at me?" I asked incredulously. Depweg lost it then and rolled on his back, kicking all four paws into the air while barks of laughter escaped his throat. "Bad dog! That's a bad dog!"

Depweg paid me no mind as he continued his mirth-filled laughing riot.

I rolled onto my stomach and pushed myself up with a grumble of annoyance interlaced with embarrassment.

I took the few steps to the hole, ignoring the asshole werewolf nearby, and dropped to my knees to allow for more accurate aiming.

"Once again: Geronimo!" I said rather than shouted as I pointed my hands down and leaned forward to fall into the hole . . . only to get friggin' caught at the waist because of my huge single ab muscle.

Through the water-filled tube, I thought I could hear the howling of laughter from someone that had better not have been Depweg . . .

Sucking in my stomach—I mean ab—and kicking my legs, I willed bloodclaws at the end of my fingers and began finding purchase down the metal tube, yanking myself a few inches at a time. I might have been grumbling to myself the entire way down through the water main.

After an amount of time that I couldn't quantify (time management had never been my strong suit), I made it to a split in the line, judging by what my exploring fingers told me. It was pitch black, even for my preter-eyes. The water blurring my eyes also didn't help much.

Once I felt the split that separated into two smaller pipes, each half the diameter of the one I was currently in, I decided this was just as good a place as any to make my entrance.

Using my bloodclaws, I latched onto a portion of the line and began tearing it apart, sending water spewing to the floor of whatever room I was about to enter. I only hoped the water wouldn't pull me from the tube to land ungracefully on my ass.

So, as the water ungracefully pulled me from the tube to land ungracefully on my ass, I looked up at the light bulb in its metal cage that hung from the ceiling . . . and spit another string of water like a fountain.

"At least Depweg didn't see this," I said to myself.

As the last of the water spilled into the room and disappeared down a grate built into the concrete floor, I did a quick, high-pitched whistle that I hoped only my werewolf friend would hear.

In answer, the tube began rocking back and forth in place. After a few minutes, I got to witness a magic trick as an enormous wet werewolf crawled through the same damn tube I had barely managed to squeeze through. Looking down, I poked my belly once and thought maybe it wasn't an ab after all.

Once Depweg landed on the floor, we began making our way through the empty corridors. I couldn't sense any soldiers down here, but could make out a light hint of perfume that teased its existence on my nostrils.

"Smell that?"

Depweg nodded once, his own nostrils flaring.

"Lead on. Your sense of smell is better than mine."

Depweg oriented down a hallway and carefully made his way forward, his nose a few inches off the ground.

We made it past a door on the left, and were about to head to the last one at the end of the hall when Depweg stopped and sniffed the air again.

Turning back to the door we had just passed, he smelled the air and then looked up at me.

"Right," I said as I grabbed the door handle and quietly opened it, expecting some sort of booby trap. "Heh, booby," I said aloud, prompting Depweg to look at me. "Sorry," I quickly added.

The room was clearly a tight office that was barely big enough to fit a desk and three chairs; two in front of the wooden desk and one behind. Past that was another door with a light that spilled from beneath. There was movement.

I placed my hand on the doorknob and opened it with a quick yank while Depweg and I sprang into the room, ready to attack.

In the room, sitting directly in front of us, was Adolf Hitler and the limp body of a woman. The man sitting next to her was rubbing her hair as he held her.

"Hitler! We've come for you!" I said in my most creepy voice while letting my eyes glow red. Depweg growled next to me while staring with fierce yellow orbs at the king of the Nazis.

"He said you'd come," Hitler spoke, defeat in his voice. There was something else that bugged me, though: acceptance. It was much more fun when my prey was scared, especially if they deserved to be hunted.

"Who?" I asked, stepping forward and keeping my eyes glowing.

"It doesn't matter. Do what you've come to do, abomination."

"Well, this is no fun," I said, letting my eyes go from a glowing red to a dark crimson. "Can't you at least pretend to be afraid and, I don't know, beg or something?"

"Would it do any good?" the man asked while gently setting the woman against the back of the couch. There was foam coming from her mouth, and I understood she had been poisoned. The room smelled lightly of almonds.

"Well, no, but it would be fun, at least." An idea came to me and I pulled the Walther pistol out of my pocket and looked at it. I knew it wouldn't do anything to me and wouldn't serve to do anything more than inconvenience Depweg . . . so why not?

I tossed the gun to him, watching as it landed with a dull thud on the couch next to him.

"Pick it up," I commanded.

Hitler looked at the weapon for a moment, and then did as I instructed.

"Point it at me and know nothing will stop our vengeance, mortal."

Hitler pointed the gun at me with a calm expression that looked tired with the weight of defeat.

Letting my eyes glow again as I took a slow step forward, I eerily announced, "We are going to tear you limb from limb. Your agony will be legendary. History books will tell how—"

Hitler smoothly brought the gun to his temple and squeezed the trigger without a moment's hesitation. There was a loud pop that was exacerbated by the tight quarters we were in as his body went limp. Blood trickled from the dime-sized hole in his temple while the exit wound oozed voraciously.

I stood frozen with my mouth still primed to finish my monologue while I slowly turned to meet Depweg's gaze. His annoyed, disappointed eyes said it all. The sonofabitch had taken our joy from us.

I slowly raised an index finger to point at the corpse, and said, "That . . . that still counts. W-We killed Hitler. Agreed?"

Depweg continued to stare at me for a few moments longer before shaking his head in disbelief and turning to make his way back to the hallway.

I looked at the man who had caused such indescribable horrors, and felt a pang of anger that he would never suffer like he should have.

With a scowl, I turned and followed after Depweg, who had found the metal doors leading to the ground floor above us. With a few switches and maybe a little bit of force here and there, we made our way outside just as dawn was threatening to crest the horizon.

"I really wanted to drink that bastard, slowly," I said to Depweg. He didn't respond, probably still mad at me for giving the coward the method of robbing the world of justice. "At least he can't hurt anyone anymore," I said in solemn acceptance, searching for the silver lining in the black clouds. "Oh, and he's definitely in Hell now. So that's neat."

Depweg's eyes turned to the horizon that was beginning to glow an ominous orange and then looked at me expectantly. It hadn't taken him long to figure out my complete lack of time management skills.

"Yeah, I know. Time to sleep," I admitted, crossing my arms and looking around. "The Allies will be here soon enough, anyway. What will you do?"

In answer, Depweg took off at a sprint, away from the sound of in-coming tanks and other military vehicles of the approaching good guys.

"Right behind you, buddy," I said to my were friend as I gave one last look around Berlin, knowing the world would be a much better place after today. The word would spread, and the Axis would fall.

"Enjoy Hell, Hitler," I snickered to myself at making a play on words on the standard Nazi greeting. Then I was sprinting to catch up with my werewolf best friend.

THE LAST FRIDAY
AN ALEX ASCHER SHORT STORY

DEVIN HANSON

This story takes place after *Lilin's Wrath*, book 4 of the Halfblood Legacy.

Chapter 1

It was the end of September in Los Angeles, and the summer heat was brutal. With the ley lines in the city back under control, the weather patterns had returned to normal again. If I was being totally honest with myself, I preferred the occasional unpredictable rain burst over this unrelenting, sweltering heat.

Still, my garden wouldn't take care of itself. I had a sun hat on, wide brimmed and made out of straw, not so much to avoid sunburn as to give myself the illusion of shade.

My tomatoes were loving the heat. I made my way along the raised beds, plucking weeds and checking on the rapidly ripening fruit. I picked an early bright red cherry tomato and popped it into my mouth. Sweet juice flooded my mouth and I groaned happily, letting my eyes sag shut.

"That good, huh?"

I flinched and jerked to my feet. There was a middle-aged man standing in my backyard, his hands tucked into the pockets of his linen suit. He had a panama hat on his head and sunglasses over his eyes. I glared at him, my hand reaching for the gardening fork.

"Who are you? What are you doing in my backyard?"

The man pulled off his sunglasses and folded them away into the breast pocket of his light jacket. He wasn't sweating. "Don't worry. I'm not a threat to you."

"Uh-huh." There was something about the man that dragged at my nerves. He looked entirely too… normal. He stood five-nine or five-ten, with average brown hair peeking out under his hat. There was nothing about his face that stood out to me. If I had encountered him on the street or in a crowd, I wouldn't have looked at him twice. There were no identifying characteristics about him. His eyes, nose, mouth, jawline, everything was just average and unremarkable. "You haven't answered my questions."

"Sorry." He gave me a placating smile. "You can call me John. I'm only here to help you."

"John." I sighed. "Okay. I'm listening."

"Good. Here." He reached into his pocket and took out a thin chain with a little metal pendant hanging from it.

I didn't take it, didn't even reach out a hand toward it. "What is it?"

"Something for a friend of yours. Sam Friday."

My brow furrowed. "Are you fae?"

"Not as such." The man bent over and laid the pendant neatly on the edge of a planter. "I would hurry, if I were you. Sam needs this."

"What is it?"

John, if that was even his name, shrugged. "Something that belongs to him."

I lifted a hand to shade my eyes from the glaring sun and leaned forward to get a better look at the pendant. It seemed to be stamped with a simple design, worn from age and use. "It doesn't look like something Sam would…"

I looked up and trailed off. My backyard was empty again.

"Damn it."

I knew I wouldn't find John, but I took a turn around the garden anyway. Sure enough, I didn't find him hiding behind the cucumber trellis or anywhere else. I went back to the tomatoes and crouched down next to the pendant. There was a patina of rust on its face. It was made out of iron, not something a fae creature would willingly hold.

Gingerly, I picked up the chain and held it up to get a closer look at it. The pendant was stamped with a cross on one side and what looked like laurel leaves on the other. Whatever it was, it was Old with a capital O. I wouldn't be surprised if I learned that it was a thousand years old or older.

Despite my caution, my curiosity was piqued. John had said the pendant belonged to Sam. Well, if that was the case, maybe Sam could shed some light for me. I abandoned my plan to spend the afternoon in the garden and went inside.

Industrial air conditioning washed over me and I paused, enjoying the feeling. The skin on my arms pebbled as my sweat cooled. I gave a little shiver and hung my sun hat up by the door, then gave Sam a call.

After a handful of rings, Sam's phone went to voice mail.

"Hi, you've reached Detective Sam Friday. If it's an emergency, call 9-1-1. I'm not able to answer the phone right now. Leave me a message, and I'll get back to you as soon as I can."

I hung up and redialed. Once again, it went to voice mail. I frowned. That wasn't like Sam. I hung up again and called the Department of Special Investigations dispatch.

"You've reached the DSI," a cheerful woman's voice greeted me. "How can I help you?"

"Hi, Sandra, it's Alex. Sam's not answering his phone. Do you know what's happening?"

"Hello, Alex! That's strange. I saw him not ten minutes ago as he was heading out the door. He didn't seem in a hurry."

"Try his radio for me? Something might be going on."

"Oh. Nothing bad, I hope?"

I tried to shake the feeling of dread creeping up the back of my neck. "I don't know. I hope not."

"Well, give me a moment. I'll raise his radio."

Sandra put me on hold, and I tried not to fidget as I listened to the scratchy classical music. I'd never been on a phone system where the music actually sounded good. Even if it wasn't horribly broken up and filled with static, the selection of music was awful. I guess if the music bored everyone equally, nobody could complain.

It didn't take long before Sandra picked up the phone again. "This is odd, Alex. I wasn't able to get him on the radio." There was worry in her voice. "I hope it's not another fae incursion."

"It shouldn't be. Can you put me through to Lara? She might know where Sam is."

"Of course. One moment."

Ten minutes later, I was on my scooter and heading for Glendale. Lara hadn't known where Sam was, only that he had mentioned that today was the anniversary of his parents' death. With a little digging, she had found where they had been buried: Forest Lawn.

Traffic through Los Angeles was always pretty miserable. Even on a Saturday like today, you could expect slows on every major freeway.

Fortunately, my little Vespa didn't go much faster than sixty miles an hour anyway, and when the traffic started to congest, I could split lanes. I had the money for a real motorcycle, but so far hadn't made it out to a dealer. It was high on my to-do list, though. I wanted something with a little power behind it for a change.

I made good time to Forest Lawn and did a circuit through the parking lot, looking for Sam's police-issued SUV. It didn't take long to find it. Even though it was a Saturday, the parking lot was almost empty. I guess people waited until Sunday to visit the graves of their loved ones.

I claimed the parking spot next to Sam's vehicle and climbed off. I was wearing a leather jacket despite the heat, and now that I wasn't riding, sweat immediately broke out across my forehead. I unzipped the jacket but left it on. I was wearing my dagger in its sheath under my arm, and I needed the jacket to keep it concealed. Leaving the dagger behind wasn't an option.

Now that I knew where Sam was, some of the urgency had left me. I took a moment to call in to DSI dispatch and report my progress.

It was time to find Sam. Forest Lawn was huge. It's over a mile across from corner to corner, with several hundred thousand graves. There were several clusters of buildings housing mausoleums and crypts, a museum, a cathedral, and dozens of walled semiprivate plots. Trying to find Sam here was going to be difficult.

I didn't know where to start looking. I called Sam on the off chance that he would pick up, and heard his ringtone coming from nearby. I had a few seconds of relief before I followed the sound back to his SUV and saw his phone sitting on the console.

Shit. I hung up and put my phone away. Why hadn't he taken his phone with him? Lara hadn't been able to find out where Sam's parents had been buried or if they had been interred in a mausoleum or what. I squinted up at the sky, pure blue from horizon to horizon. Maybe there was a directory I could look in.

Next to the parking lot was the museum, with the cathedral adjacent. One of those places was likely to have the answers I needed. I didn't think Sam's parents were famous enough to make it into a museum listing, so I headed for the cathedral.

My mother was Mahlat bat Lilith, Succubus of Lust and responsible for the sin of lust among mankind. Since turning twenty-one, I was not welcome on consecrated ground. The last time I had accidentally stepped onto cathedral grounds, it had felt like my skin had burst into flames. That wasn't to say all churches and religious buildings were built on hallowed ground; modern religious practices didn't always keep up with the old rituals. For a place the size of Forest Lawn, I had hope that the priests had better things to do with their time.

Still, I was cautious as I approached the cathedral. There was a wide set of concrete steps leading up to a brick plaza in front of the cathedral, and I took them one at a time, feeling ahead of me with an outstretched hand.

At the top step, I still hadn't felt anything, so I moved forward onto the plaza. Agony stabbed up my arm and I yelped. I stumbled backward and almost fell down the steps. My hand had been burned to a crisp in the brief moment of exposure.

Whimpering in pain, I clutched my seared hand to my stomach and backed down to the curb. Already I could feel the burning tingle of my cracked and blistered flesh healing. The air smelled like barbecue around me as I sat down on the curb and clenched my teeth to keep from sobbing out loud.

It didn't take long for my hand to heal, but it had felt like an hour. When the pain had subsided enough for me to straighten up again, the skin of my hand had healed almost back to normal once more. My hand was pink to the wrist, as if I had dipped it into a pot of boiling water. Blackened curls of flesh flaked away, revealing the healing skin beneath.

Disgusted, I brushed the mess off my lap and picked it out from between my fingers. My clothes were stained where I had hugged my injured hand to my stomach, as if I had dumped a plate of grilled chicken on myself.

Voices sounded behind me, coming from the plaza. I tucked my still-healing hand into my jacket out of sight and turned my head away. The last thing I wanted was someone coming over and asking me if I was all right.

"—know where he is. No, I told you already. He left his phone in his car! We can't track him if..." The man's voice trailed off, sounding frustrated.

I could hear the indistinct buzz of someone screaming over the phone. Even without it being on speaker, I could hear the anger.

"Oh. There's a website? Yeah. Uh-huh. Wess, check the website, see if you can find the grave. Uh-huh. No, Wess is searching for it."

The two men walked past me and I lifted my head just far enough to sneak a peek. They were tough-looking thugs, heavy with muscle. One of them looked like he had been dipped in tattoo ink, the designs crude and faded. I could recognize prison tattoos when I saw them, and that guy had to have spent a significant portion of his adult life behind bars.

Tattoo had his phone pressed against his head, and he half turned to look at Wess. "How's it coming?"

"Got it," Wess nodded. "Sunrise Slope, lot 1338, space 1A."

"Yeah, Wess found the grave. We're on our way now."

I watched the two men cross the parking lot and head off into the manicured grounds of the cemetery. Once they were out of sight, I stood up and checked on my hand. It was back to normal once more, if still tingly when I flexed my fingers.

What were the odds that Tattoo and Wess were talking about Sam? I got my phone out, and without much trouble, found Forest Lawn's website. Sure enough, there was a tool to search for a specific grave. I put in "Janet and Paul Friday," and their grave location popped up.

The location for Sam's parents' grave was the same given by Wess. I touched the comforting weight of my dagger under my arm, then set off after the two thugs. Whatever business they had with Sam, I wanted to be nearby to help in case he needed it.

I crossed the parking lot at a trot, then slowed to a walk once I reached the edge of the asphalt. Even that slight exertion had sweat running down between my shoulder blades. Gingerly, I reached a hand over the curb, hoping that the consecration rites hadn't been carried out over the whole cemetery.

Nothing happened, and I let out a sigh of relief. Being my mother's daughter was great and all, but sometimes the side effects made me question if it was worth it.

Just stepping off the asphalt and onto the grass made it feel ten degrees cooler. I saw Wess and Tattoo up ahead of me, climbing the slowly rolling hill. They were already almost a hundred yards away. It would be suspicious if I followed directly after them, so I aimed for a spot a little to the left, then I ducked my head down and picked up the pace.

Forest Lawn was beautiful. If it weren't for the rows and rows of graves, it would be the best park in Los Angeles. Old-growth trees towered overhead, providing pools of deep shade to break up the unrelenting sun. It was also completely empty. Besides the two men ahead of me, I hadn't seen a single person in the whole cemetery. The ground undulated subtly, and the two thugs went out of sight for a bit every few minutes. I didn't worry about it that much. The graves we were heading for were over a quarter of a mile away. Even at my fast walk, I wouldn't get close for another few minutes.

I cleared a rise and glanced to my right, trying to be subtle about searching for my quarry. I didn't see them, but there were plenty of folds in the ground for them to be obscured by. I angled a little bit to the right to close the distance some.

The thugs didn't reappear. I looked around, wondering if I had misestimated how far I had come. Then shadows shifted at the base of the tree ahead of me, and Wess and Tattoo stepped out from around the trunk of a massive live oak.

"Looking for something, miss?" Tattoo sneered at me.

Shit. I tried on a smile. "Oh, hi! Sorry, you startled me."

Tattoo walked toward me, his arms spread to the sides. "Didn't your mother tell you not to walk around a park alone? You never know who you might run into."

"My mother is dead," I said. "I'm just trying to visit her grave."

"Aw, so sad." Wess shook his head and got his phone out. "What's her name? Maybe we can help you find it."

As far as I knew, my mother didn't have a grave. Still, I had to tell them something. "Sandra. Sandra Halsin. It's very kind of you to help me. I've always come to visit her with my father, but he isn't feeling well this year. I was hoping to just head in the general direction then find my way when I got close."

"Makes sense," Wess said. "Except, I'm not finding any Sandra Halsins in the directory. Maybe you got the name wrong?"

"It's her mother, Wess," Tattoo chuckled. "Pretty sure she hasn't forgotten what her name is. Unless… you aren't here for her."

"You sure you spelled it right?" I asked. "It's Sandra, with an a."

Tattoo was only a few yards away now, and I felt the waft of lust coming off him. "He knows how to spell Sandra, girl. What's your name, then?"

"Alexandra," I said. "Maybe the last name is wrong, then? Check it again with a different spelling?"

"Nah," Wess leered at me. He put his phone away and joined Tattoo, his arms folded over his chest. Of the two, Wess had broader shoulders, like he spent more time at the gym. The lust was coming off him stronger than from his companion.

"Oh. I have to ask. Do you have a form of photo ID on you?" I smiled brightly at Tattoo.

"Why?" Tattoo's face scrunched up in a puzzled frown.

"It'll help the police identify your body."

For a long moment, the two thugs stared at me in confused disbelief. Then Wess's face darkened in anger. "You cheeky little bitch," he growled and swung a punch at my head.

I ducked to the side and felt the wind of his fist as it went by. I straightened up and punched him in the gut. I'd been taking lessons, and I could feel the punch land with brutal force. Wess's feet almost left the ground, then he folded over and collapsed like a pile of wet laundry.

42

Wess dry retched and struggled for breath. I kicked him in the ribs, then jumped back as Tattoo charged at me with a yell. Brass glinted in the sun, and I saw Tattoo had slipped on a set of knuckles. I tried to get out of the way, but a gravestone caught my heel and I stumbled.

Tattoo crashed into me, and we went tumbling to the grass. He had to weigh three hundred pounds or more, and he landed squarely on top of me. Thanks to my heritage from Mahlat, having Tattoo drop his full weight on my chest only knocked the air out of me a little bit. He started raining heavy blows down onto my head, the brass knuckles giving his fists additional bruising force.

He hadn't managed to pin my arms when he'd tackled me, and I raised them to shield my face. Blows smashed down onto my arms and I twisted, trying to find a way to shift his weight. I didn't have the leverage to move him, even though I possessed the brute strength to pick him off the ground.

A punch slipped through my guard, and the brass knuckles connected with my temple. My vision flew apart, pain stabbing through my head. I felt my arms get slapped aside, and a second punch crashed into my jaw.

The fight puddled out of me and Tattoo grunted in satisfaction. "That's right, bitch." He pushed himself to his feet and swung a kick into my stomach. I rolled away from him, trying to pull myself together. "You just stay down, now. I'll deal with you in a sec."

I heard Tattoo walk over to where Wess was groaning on the ground. I was already feeling better, but I stayed where I was until the earth stopped spinning in slow circles around me. Then I climbed upright and spat blood from my split lip on the ground. I tested the inside of my lip with my tongue and found nothing but smooth skin once more.

"Hey!" I snapped.

Tattoo jerked around and stared at me. "What? How did—"

I jumped at him and he threw a punch wildly, more panicked than considered. I ducked and hammered a blow into his kidney, making Tattoo gasp and twist away. I kicked him in the knee and heard a pop.

Tattoo yelped and fell to the grass, clutching his knee. I gave him the same kick he had given me, and he rolled onto his side with a groan.

"Who's the bitch now?"

"You wrecked my knee, you stupid whore!"

I kicked him onto his stomach and knelt down on his back. He reached for my leg, so I grabbed his wrist and twisted it around behind him. I forced his hand up toward his shoulder blades until he stopped struggling, then grabbed the hair at the back of his head and pulled back until I could see his eyes.

"What do you want with Sam Friday?" I demanded.

"I'm not telling you shit!" Tattoo grunted.

"Wrong answer." I pulled his wrist up a few inches higher, until I felt the tendons in his shoulder creak. "Another inch and you're going to be left-handed. Talk."

"Fine!" Tattoo let out a sob through his clenched teeth. "We were told to collect him."

"You know he's a cop, right? Trying a stunt like that is going to earn you hard time." I eased off the pressure on his wrist a little. "Where were you going to bring him?"

"Doesn't matter that he's a cop," Tattoo muttered. "He's a Friday."

That raised my eyebrows. "What's his family got to do with this?"

"You don't know?" He twisted around as far as he could and looked up at me. "Who the hell are you, anyway?"

"Answer the question," I said, and forced his wrist back up to the limit.

"Screw you," Tattoo gritted out.

"Last chance. I've heard jerking off with the wrong hand isn't nearly as much fun."

Tattoo didn't respond. I tightened my grip on his hair and twisted his head around. His eyes were rolled back in his head. A tremor ran through him, and the tension in his shoulders relaxed. I got off him in a hurry and stood over him for a moment, unsure of what to do.

Gingerly, I nudged him onto his back with my foot. There was foam oozing from his open mouth. I knelt down and pressed my fingers to his neck. Nothing. He was dead. I swallowed and realized I couldn't hear Wess's groaning anymore. I went to check on him and found the same foam dripping from his slack mouth.

Poison. Probably a capsule tooth. Tattoo had killed himself rather than reveal what his intentions with Sam had been.

Shit. Sam. I left the thugs where they lay and broke into a run.

CHAPTER 2

I found Sam standing over a grave, his head bowed and a sheaf of roses dangling from one hand. He looked up as I came running up the hill toward him and raised a hand in a half wave.

"Alex? What are you doing here?"

I slowed to a stop as I reached him and panted for breath. Sweat soaked into my shirt, but it was the last thing on my mind. "Sam, thank God you're all right. Why'd you leave your phone in your car, huh?"

"I wanted some privacy. Speaking of… how did you find me?"

"I followed a couple thugs from the parking lot. Sam, we've got to go."

"Thugs, huh?" Sam did a turn, pointedly looking at the empty cemetery around us. "Where?"

"They committed suicide instead of answering my questions," I growled. "Come on, Sam!"

Alarm flashed over his face. "What?! Okay." He took a step away, then remembered he was holding flowers. He turned back and squatted down. Sam reached out a hand, pressing it against the grave at his feet, then put the flowers down. "Right. You better show me the bodies."

I wanted to drag Sam back to his SUV, by the collar if I had to, but I knew he would insist on playing this by the book. "All right. They're not far away; five minutes or so."

As I jogged back to where I had left Tattoo and Wess, I tried to question Sam without giving away what answers I was trying to get to.

"What did your parents do, Sam?" I asked between trying to find my breath.

"Uh, well, my dad was an accountant at a bank. My mom was a portrait painter." Sam hadn't just sprinted a quarter of a mile, so his breath came easily.

That didn't sound like the Fridays had been involved in some sort of secret organization, though both of those professions sounded almost suspiciously mundane. "I don't think you've ever told me how they died."

"Car accident," he said shortly.

My own father had died in a "car accident." I wanted to probe more, but Sam's tone made it clear he wasn't interested in discussing it. "Oh. Well, what little I got out of the thugs suggested they were interested in you because of your family, not because you're a cop."

"I don't know why they would be. My parents weren't anyone special."

"This isn't, like, a revenge thing for something your father did?"

I slowed down from my jog and stopped. We were in the spot I had left Tattoo and Wess in, but the bodies were nowhere in sight.

"Alex, the real world isn't like your life. My dad managed mortgage loans. He didn't have any enemies. Why did we stop?"

"This is the spot. Or I think it is. What about your mother?"

"Yes. The horde of angry mobsters furious about their portraits." Sam rolled his eyes. "I don't see any bodies."

"They were here. I swear."

"Maybe you got the wrong place?"

I glared at Sam, but had to admit he might be right. The scenery at Forest Lawn could get repetitive, especially in this part where all the headstones were plaques flush with the ground. "Maybe? I guess it's possible."

"Let's spread out and look around."

"Absolutely not. I'm staying with you."

Sam sighed. "Fine. Let's get this over with."

We spent the next ten minutes wandering around the area, but all it did was cement in my mind that we had been in the right spot to begin with. Finally, I called off our search.

"Someone must have moved them." I flapped my jacket, trying to get some air circulation to my damp shirt.

"You're sure they were dead?"

I scowled at him, trying not to get angry. "I'm not a doctor, but I think I can tell when someone's dead. No pulse, foaming at the mouth. I had the guy's arm twisted up between his shoulder blades; it must have hurt like hell, but he just went limp. I almost dislocated his arm before I let go. You don't do that if you're pretending."

Sam muttered a curse and frowned around at the trees. "It's not April first, is it? You're not going to start laughing?"

"It's September, Sam," I gave him a wry smile. "Sorry, I don't think my friends being hunted is a laughing matter."

"So, they were after me because of my family?"

"Yeah." I nodded, relieved. "Tattoo said he was interested in you because you were a Friday."

"That'd be my mother's side of the family, then." He grinned at the puzzled look on my face. "My dad took her name when they married. She was an only child and didn't want the family name to die. I'm the last Friday."

"That's… enlightened of him. Can we talk on the way back to the parking lot?"

"Yeah." Sam frowned back in the direction of his parents' grave, then shook his head. "Feels like someone is watching me. Let's get out of here."

I nodded and turned to lead the way. "Tell me about your mother, then?"

"What is there to say? She didn't make much of a living on her paintings, though she was really good at it. There's not much of a market for portraiture these days. She spent most of her time being a housewife."

"I'm not trying to tarnish your memories of her or anything, but I have to ask. Is there a possibility she had a second life that she was hiding from you?"

It was a while before Sam responded. We had covered nearly half the ground back to the parking lot before he sighed and shrugged. "I can't see it. Mom was the fun-loving one in the family. Always planning day trips and finding ways to get us out of the house on the weekend. If anyone could have had a secret life, it was my dad. He never talked about his work in detail, and I always just assumed that it was tedious and boring. He made pretty good money doing his job. Enough that we were never wanting."

It was hard for me not to feel jealous. My childhood had been the polar opposite of that. What I wouldn't have given to have had a happy childhood with parents that cared about me. "How about your grandparents, then? On your mother's side."

Sam shrugged again. "I didn't really know them that well. They retired before I was born. I saw them every few years during the holidays, and once on a summer trip to Hawaii. I think they lived in Europe somewhere. They passed when I was in high school."

"Were they religious?"

"I guess? Maybe? I think we went to church a few times. My parents definitely weren't."

We reached the parking lot. I had cooled off after my run, but stepping out into the unfiltered sunlight made me start to sweat again. Sam's SUV and my scooter were the only vehicles present. I walked him over to his SUV, and he got in and rolled down the window.

"I'll see you back at the precinct?" he asked.

I leaned against the door and got out the pendant from my pocket. I held it out to him. "I think this is yours."

He took it and frowned. "No, I don't think so." He turned it over in his hand and held it up so the light caught the cross side of the pendant. "Is this why you asked if they were religious? Where'd you get this thing, anyway?"

"I don't know. Someone appeared in my garden this morning and handed it to me. Said you needed it."

"I'm guessing you're not using 'appeared' as a euphemism."

"Not this time." I reached out and folded Sam's hands around the pendant. "Hold onto that. I don't know what's going on, but we'll figure it out."

"Should I wear it?"

I hesitated before shaking my head. "Better not. Until we know what it is, putting it on might have unexpected consequences."

Sam snorted. "You're not good at being comforting." He slipped the pendant into a pocket.

I patted the door and backed up. "I'll be right behind you. See you at the precinct."

Traffic to the precinct wasn't bad, but there was still enough that I was able to stay on Sam's tail the whole way there. I followed him into the precinct parking lot, and then downstairs to where the DSI had their office in the basement.

The Department of Special Investigations wasn't held in high regard among the general LAPD. Most viewed them as little better than the X-files: crackpots chasing figments of their imagination. The lieutenant of the DSI, Lara Moreno, had enough of a reputation that she had managed to push the new department through the planning phase and into actual reality. After a series of successfully solved cases, the newly inaugurated department had been cemented as a necessary part of the Los Angeles' peacekeeping force, in the eyes of the chief of police if nobody else.

The DSI didn't have a lot of officers assigned to it. Most of the time, there was enough going on in the city to keep everyone out of the office. Today, it was empty except for the dispatch, Sandra, and Officer Davis sitting in the corner, absorbed in his computer work. He didn't even look up when we walked in.

Sandra gave me a wide smile and waved to Sam. "Hey, there you are, Detective Friday! I'm glad Alex was able to find you."

"Hello, Sandra. Any messages?"

"Other than half the department freaking out about you going radio silent, no."

Sam scratched his head and gave her a wry grin. "Sorry. Just wanted some privacy. I suppose I should have told someone where I was going."

"Next time, Detective, it would be appreciated. Don't go anywhere. Lieutenant Moreno wanted to talk to you before you left again."

"Yep. Thanks for the heads-up, Sandra."

She waved again, and we headed back to the little room that served Sam as an office. It wasn't much bigger than a closet: enough room for a little desk with a computer and two chairs. It was claustrophobic with the door closed, so I left it open.

"Busted," I grinned at him.

He rolled a shoulder. "It happens. As happy as I am to be sharing my office with you, did you have a reason for following me down here? I'm not going to get jumped by thugs at the precinct."

"Don't you want to find out why they were interested in you?"

Sam grunted. "I suppose. It wasn't high on my priority list. Is that what you're going to do now?"

"We," I corrected him. "We are going to do it now. And I have a feeling that pendant is the key to all this."

"So long as we stay here, I'm game."

"Let's start with the pendant, then," I suggested.

Sam pulled the thin chain out of his pocket and set the pendant on the table. "Doesn't look like much. A cross on this side, and," he flipped it over, "What is that? A laurel crown?"

"Could be. That's what I thought it was."

"It's so small. I can't make out much detail." He opened his desk drawer and got out a sheet of notebook paper and a pencil. "Maybe a rubbing will show more."

I should have thought of making a rubbing myself, but in my defense, I'd had other things on my mind. Sam knew what he was doing. He did a series of rubbings for each side of the pendant at various pencil pressures, then scanned it into his computer. Using imaging software, he played with the rubbings until he had a composite picture of each side.

"Nine leaves on one side and eleven on the other," I observed. "Normally they're even, right?"

"I guess. It'll make it easier to search for it. I'm more interested in the other side. I didn't see any writing, but there were words there at some point." He pointed at the vague smudges along the top and bottom of the pendant on the cross side. "I can't make them out, though."

I got up from my chair so I could look over Sam's shoulder. He was right. "Ad… something, something, there's an E in there, I think. Definitely an M or two on the bottom."

"Doesn't narrow it down much," Sam grunted. "Can't even count the number of letters or if there is more than two words."

"Yeah, but there's still something to go on. Check to see if—"

There was a knock on the doorframe and I looked over to see Sandra leaning in. "The Lieutenant's back," she said. "And there's a visitor for you, Detective."

"Thanks, Sandra," Sam said. He got up from the computer and I had to back into a corner of the little office to make room. "I'll check in with the boss, then we can keep working on this," he told me.

"Sure." I followed Sam out into the open general office and saw Lara standing by her office. There was a man with her, his back turned to us.

Lara saw me come out behind Sam, and the stern look on her face softened marginally. "Detective Friday, I want you in my office when you're done out here."

"Yes, ma'am," Sam replied. He started walking around the cluster of desks toward the newcomer. "Hi, I'm Detective Friday. How can I help you?"

The man turned to look at Sam, and I saw the tattoos on his neck peeking out from under his button-up shirt. "Adverse sun time," he said.

Sam hesitated, slowing to a stop still five or six paces from the man. "What was that?"

I had a different angle than Sam did, and I saw the man's hand reaching around to the small of his back. There was something deliberate about the motion that grabbed my eye. "Sam!" I shouted. "Gun!"

Sam's eyes flicked to the man's waist, then he threw himself sideways behind the cover of the desks. The man's hand came up holding a compact pistol and he fired rapidly, trying to track Sam. The gunshots hammered at my ears, deafeningly loud in the closed space. Clouds of splintered wood exploded into the air, and ricochets whined.

I ripped the dagger free from under my jacket. The man swung the gun toward me and I threw the dagger as hard as I could. Muzzle flashed, and an impact hammered into my shoulder. It felt like someone had swung a sledgehammer at me, and I staggered. More shots rang out, then the room fell quiet.

Lara's door banged open and the lieutenant stepped out, gun held in front of her in both hands. I picked myself up off the floor and lunged up on top of the clustered desks, ready to throw myself at the man.

The fight was over. The man was leaning back against the wall, staring down at the hilt of my dagger protruding from his chest. The gun in his hand was locked open on an empty magazine.

"Drop the weapon!" Lara snarled.

The man's head swung around to look at Lara, his face confused. Then clarity returned and his jaw clenched. He dropped the empty gun and held his hands up. He coughed, and flecks of foam spilled from his lips. Then his knees gave out and he slid to the ground.

Lara covered him with her gun as I picked my way over the desks and dropped down next to Sam. "You okay?"

"I'm fine," Sam snapped. "Deal with that prick!"

I left Sam and circled around to stand next to Lara. My dagger had sunk nearly to the hilt in his chest. It had been a lucky throw. The blade wasn't balanced for throwing, but the afternoons spent in my backyard tossing it at a sheet of plywood seemed to have paid off. I put my boot against his chest and yanked the dagger free.

"You're hit," Lara said.

I glanced down at my shoulder and muttered a curse. I stuck a finger through the fresh hole in my jacket and felt the healed skin beneath. I hadn't even felt the pain of the gunshot through the adrenaline. "Went clear through," I said irritably. "I just had this jacket cleaned, too."

I heard footsteps coming at a run and slipped the bloody dagger back under my jacket. I'd pay for that later when I had to spend an hour cleaning the sheath, but better that than spending the rest of the day in a cell.

A pair of uniformed officers burst into the room and Lara stepped forward. "It's over," she said loudly and held up her badge for the two uniforms to see. "We've got everything under control."

The uniforms holstered their weapons and gawked around at the damage to the room for a moment before ducking back out the door again.

"Shit," Lara muttered. She looked down at the man distastefully. "You know what this is about?"

"We're working on it," I shook my head.

"Well, there goes my evening. I'll be up all night doing paperwork. Sam! Did you get hit?"

"Not this time," he grinned. "Thanks to Alex."

"Figure this out, will you? It looks bad if we have hit men walking freely into the precinct. Davis, find out how the hell he got in here with a gun, would you?"

"On it, boss." Davis grabbed his jacket and left, stepping gingerly over the slumped body blocking the aisle.

"Come on," Sam said softly. "Lara will handle cleanup."

"They gonna wonder why the guy has a knife wound in the chest?"

Sam shrugged. "He must have tripped on the way in. Honestly, someone who pulls a gun in the precinct isn't going to get much scrutiny over how they died. I'll make sure Lara routes the autopsy to Dr. Fenway. I want to know what that poison is."

"Still doubt me when I say there were two in the cemetery?"

"I never doubted you, Alex. Let's get to work."

Sam shut the door to his little office to keep the growing bustle of traffic from disturbing us. Whether he had doubted me previously or not, having a gunman show up and take a shot at him had removed any complacency from Sam's attitude. He pulled up the composite image of the pendant and stared at it, a frown on his face.

"What did that man say before he opened fire?" he asked.

"Uh." I replayed the moment in my head. "Adverse sun time, I think."

"Yeah, that's what I heard too. I'm guessing he's not talking about getting a sunburn or heatstroke."

"Those would be the worst last words ever." I dragged my chair over next to Sam's so I could sit while looking at his monitor. "Could be code for something, maybe?"

"Or we just misheard it. I'll try to run the phrase through the police database and see if I can get any hits."

"Then I'll work my Google-fu and see if I can find anything on the civilian net."

"You want to use the computer? Phone reception down here is pretty miserable."

"It'd help," I admitted. "Where will you be?"

"I'll be right outside. If I know Lara, the DSI is on lockdown. Nobody is getting in or out, so it should be safe enough."

I nodded. "Keep an ear open anyway."

"I will, don't you worry about that."

We swapped places and Sam left to use one of the workstations outside his office. It wouldn't be a bad idea to do an image search myself. Maybe I could find something on the internet that could point at who these thugs were.

I quickly found that my initial thought that having an uneven number of leaves on the crown would make it stand out was correct. I knew of a few organizations that had laurel leaves in their emblems, and the number of leaves was significant.

Unfortunately, searching for conspiracies with "nine" and "eleven" in them was a deep, dark rabbit hole. Every crackpot with access to a computer had posted their pet theories about the two towers tragedy, and the internet was polluted with their nonsense. After spending almost twenty minutes clicking through heated debates about the melting point of steel beams, I gave up that route of inquiry.

The cross suggested the organization was somehow related to the Christian church. There were so many splinter groups and factions that fell under the broad umbrella of Christianity that I could spend all day researching them and still only dabble in the surface. Weren't there nine apostles or something? No, there were twelve of them.

Ugh. I hung my head and stared down at the keyboard, trying to think of a way to narrow down my search. What did I know about them? Not much, beyond that they were fanatical about keeping their secrets. Maybe an autopsy would reveal the makeup of the poison, and that would help narrow it down. There couldn't be that many compounds that killed so quickly.

Sam's pendant was sitting on the desk next to the keyboard, and I picked it up. The chain wasn't anything notable, but the pendant itself was odd. Iron wasn't often used for coins or tokens. It was too hard to strike cold, unlike copper, silver, or gold, so it required a forge in order to press the faces onto blanks. That wasn't unheard of, but it definitely implied a larger organization. Small cults a thousand years ago didn't have the resources to forge iron tokens.

It was also possible the iron was a statement against the fae. Iron and fae did not mix, and making a sigil out of iron could have been a way to guarantee a member wasn't an impostor. I sighed. None of that helped me find out who was hunting Sam, though.

The slogan was probably my best bet. I tilted the pendant under Sam's desk lamp, trying to convince my brain to understand what the worn lettering was. Sam's rubbings had brought out detail that wasn't visible to the eye, but there were patterns in the rust that hinted at the ghosts of additional letters.

I frowned thoughtfully. Combined with the rubbings, I was pretty certain that there were only two words on the pendant: one on top of the cross and one below. I could make out maybe half of the letters, but I couldn't make sense out of them. They were, I realized belatedly, probably not in English.

Sam stuck his head in the office. "Making any progress?" he asked.

"Nothing to get excited about. How about you?"

"Maybe. I was searching for tattoos that said 'adverse sun time,' and—"

"Wait. Say that again."

"Adverse sun time?"

"Say it faster. Like that guy did." Sam complied and I laughed. "That's it! It's Latin. Adversus unitum."

"I know."

Some of the elation left me. "You do?"

"Like I was trying to say, I was searching for tattoos, and the search returned that Latin phrase from a 90 percent letter match. It translates to 'united against' or something like that."

"Well, shit. Who had the tattoo?"

"A man named Robert Torn."

"Is he still alive?" Given the habit of people connected to this to end up dead, I didn't have much hope.

"He is. And we have an address."

"Road trip?" I grinned.

Sam lifted his hand from behind the door and showed me the bulletproof vest hanging from it. "Road trip."

Chapter 3

It never ceased to amaze me how diverse Los Angeles was. I wouldn't have guessed there was a run-down old shack in the middle of the city, and yet here we were. Granted, Lake View Terrace wouldn't be winning any awards for city planning, but I didn't expect it to be this… I don't know. Ghetto wasn't the right word for it.

"Rural," Sam said to himself as he eased the SUV up to a curb. A chicken squawked at us and flapped away, too fat to get off the ground.

"Are chickens even legal in LA?"

Sam opened his door and sniffed. "Do you smell goats? I don't know. I'm not current with local regulations. Probably, though. You'd be surprised what is permitted in these smaller towns."

The houses around us all had large lots, a quarter acre at least. It was shocking to see land that spacious with shabby two- or three-bedroom houses on them. Around where I lived, and for most of the rest of Los Angeles, the lots weren't much larger than the footprint of the house that sat on them. In Hollywood, lots like these had mansions on them. Or, more likely, an apartment building.

"Which house are we going to?" I asked.

"That one at the end of the street on the left." We started walking up the slight hill and Sam said, "I've been trying to understand that slogan. Who are these guys united against?"

"Right now, you."

Sam gave a rueful laugh and shook his head. "Okay. But you know what I mean. That pendant has got to be centuries old. They can't have had a vendetta against my family for that long, right?"

"I don't know, Sam. It's possible. Speaking of the pendant, you have it, right?"

He pulled it from his pocket and held it up for me to see. "Right here."

"Good. Hold onto it. I've got a feeling there's something important about it."

Sam nodded. We reached the property line of the house and he tucked the pendant away again. "How are we doing this? Police style or Alex style?"

"What's that supposed to mean?"

"I mean, are we just going in or are we knocking first?"

I rolled my eyes. "Contrary to popular belief, I don't violate the law on a regular basis."

Sam just looked at me, a slightly incredulous look on his face.

"Okay," I admitted. "Maybe sometimes. Or a lot of the times. But it's justified!"

"I didn't say otherwise," Sam grinned.

I scowled at him, trying to decide if he was making fun of me or not. "Are you really asking my opinion?"

"As far as I'm concerned, this is your bailiwick, not mine. I'll follow your lead."

"Okay. Then, let's knock and see what happens."

Sam nodded and we walked up the overgrown sidewalk. The concrete was seamed with cracks and weeds pushing through the gaps. I took the lead up to the house, listening for sounds from inside. The house was past run down. Water damage stained the stucco on the south side, and the roofline was sagging in the middle.

The front door had been green at one point, but more paint had flaked off than remained. The screen door was attached by the bottom hinge only, and hung from the doorframe heavily askew. A breeze pushed at the screen door, making it creak and groan as it shifted back and forth.

"This place looks abandoned," Sam muttered behind me.

He wasn't wrong. I knocked on the front door, and it gave under my hand. Just a tap caused it to sag open a few inches. "Hello?" I called softly.

I heard nothing but the breeze and the soft sound of Sam drawing his gun and racking the slide. I glanced back at him and gave a little shrug, then pushed the door open the rest of the way. Robert Torn was a hoarder. Tinfoil was taped over most of the windows, sinking the living room into a deep gloom. One wall was covered in newspaper clippings, with hand-scribbled notes stapled to the drywall.

The air was heavy and still, and it smelled of rats. I stepped gingerly into the house, trying to breathe shallowly. A chorus of squeaks and a rush of rustling snapped my head around, and I saw a flurry of rats fleeing from the kitchen. There was something on the ground there, partially hidden by a flimsy wheeled kitchen island.

Sam stepped in behind me and tilted his head toward the kitchen. I reached into my jacket and pulled out my dagger. It stuck for a moment, and I had to tug it free. Crusty gore stained the blade and I grimaced. Note to self: in the future, clean the blade after using it.

The dusty smell in the air thickened into a rotten funk, and I lifted the back of my wrist to my nose, trying not to gag. I stepped around the little island and turned my head away, swallowing hard against my rising gorge. An old man, presumably Robert Torn, lay on the ground. Most of his flesh had been eaten away by the rats.

"Damn," Sam sighed. "Let me guess. Mr. Torn?"

The body twitched as a rat squirmed down a pant leg. It was hugely fat, and had to struggle to make it past the ankle cuff, then it scampered into a cabinet.

"I think I'm going to be sick," I choked out.

"Sink," Sam said.

I made it to the sink and emptied my stomach.

"Got a wallet," Sam announced behind me. "It's him. My guess is he died about two weeks ago."

I spat my mouth clean. "So much for asking him questions," I rasped. "Any idea what killed him?"

"Guy was in his eighties. It's a little hard to tell now, but I think he was pretty hefty, judging by his waist size. My guess is heart disease."

"I wonder if rats would be affected by that poison they're so fond of taking." I looked around the kitchen, up at the ceiling, and the cabinets. Anywhere but at the gnawed body at my feet. "I think I'll go check out that mural our guy was working on."

"Yep." Sam squatted down and started picking through Torn's clothing with a ballpoint pen.

I left in a hurry before my stomach revolted again. Out in the living room, the smell wasn't nearly as strong, and I felt my throat start to relax. I was curious about the newspaper clippings on the wall. Unhinged conspiracy theorists loved collecting bits and pieces of information that they believed supported whatever crackpot assumption they were chasing.

I assumed Torn was the same. A lot of the clippings were yellowed with age and cigarette smoke. Whatever this was, he had been working on it for decades. The floor area in front of the wall was clear of debris. Most hoarders weren't so particular about keeping open floor space, so whatever was on the wall must have been important to Torn.

After picking my way over to the clear space, I got my phone out to use as a flashlight and swept it over the clippings closest to me. Artist Janet Friday Paints Portrait of Multimillionaire Movie Mogul. Strings led to movie ticket stubs, then to a paper coaster with a bar logo on it. Then a grainy Polaroid shot of a wedding. A preschool class photo with a little boy circled several times. A young Sam Friday holding a track trophy and grinning.

"Sam, you better get in here," I called.

"What'd you find?" Sam asked, sticking his head around the corner.

"You're popular."

"Well, I try not to brag, but…" he trailed off as he neared the wall and saw where my phone light was pointing. His high school graduation photo, complete with cap and gown. "What the hell?"

I stepped back to give him room and swept my light in the other direction, following the patchwork of threads down the wall. Photos grew less common, but the progression of Janet Friday growing up and becoming a painter was clear to see. There were other strings leading off, but I kept my focus narrowed to just the family progression.

Torn had been tracking the Friday family line for nearly sixty years. At the far end, there was a photo of Sam's great-grandparents, black and white and staring stiffly ahead. Below it was a newspaper article old enough that the hand-set print blocks were evident. Only the headline was still legible, the rest faded away to dusty smudges.

"Lord Friday Abdicates Title," I read aloud. "Did you know your family was noble?"

"I had no idea." Sam walked over to stand next to me. He had a stubby little LED flashlight that was like five times as bright as my phone, and he swept it around, taking in the whole of the mural. "This guy has been stalking my family for years. Is all this because of some old claim to power or something?"

"Your guess is as good as mine."

"I'm not going to lie," Sam swallowed. "This whole thing has me feeling kind of violated."

I nodded sympathetically. "What do you want to do with it all?"

He frowned. "Part of me wants to destroy it, but another part of me is curious. Torn knew more about my family than my mother did. I'm certain of that. We'll never find what they want with me if I don't start learning myself."

"I agree. But it's up to you."

"It'd take a CSI team a week to unravel all this." Sam leaned in to peer at one of the faded newspaper clippings. "Assuming they'd be able to make heads or tails of this mess."

I opened my mouth to reply and heard an engine roar to life outside on the street. A moment later, the front window shattered. Brilliant sunlight streamed in, blinding me, and I flinched. There was a secondary smash of glass, and a sudden rush of heat rolled over me.

Out in the street, a pickup truck squealed away from the curb. The reek of cheap alcohol stung my nose, and in seconds, the floor of the living room was a sea of licking blue flames. The stacked newspapers and junk ignited instantly, and clouds of acrid smoke filled the air. Already, the front door was blocked by a growing inferno.

"We have to go through the back!" I shouted.

Sam was staring at the mural. "I just need to…" He started fumbling in his pocket for his phone, and I grabbed his arm.

"No time, Sam! Move!"

I dragged him away from the wall and into the kitchen; flames were already leaping to the ceiling in the living room. I jumped Torn's body and ran for the back door, grabbing the knob and finding it was locked. Smoke swirled around me, stinging at my eyes and searing my lungs. I fumbled the deadbolt open and pulled. It didn't move.

"Let me," Sam gasped. He grabbed the doorknob and strained, and it broke off in his hand. "Shit!"

I could feel the heat behind me. The roar and crackle of the fire was spreading, climbing through the peeling wallpaper and hungrily searching for fuel. I knocked Sam aside and ran at the door, dropping my shoulder at the last moment. I bounced off uselessly. I didn't weigh enough to smash through the door that way.

"The window?" Sam asked, pointing to the little window over the sink. It was too small for Sam to fit through easily.

In response, I drew back my hand and punched the door as hard as I could. Wood splintered under my fist and pain stabbed up my wrist. My knuckles were bloody and split, but I ignored the pain and slammed my fist into the door again and again. I put all my strength into the effort, drawing on the supernatural power of my succubus side.

One of the door panels finally broke free. Fresh air flowed past me and I heard the fire roar in response. A wave of heat rolled over me. I reached through the opening and grabbed the partially splintered upright stile.

I braced myself against the jamb and pulled as hard as I could. With a final cry of effort, I ripped the door in half before Sam grabbed me around the waist and dived through the remains of the door, sending us tumbling through the overgrown weeds. I fetched up against a stack of tires and climbed to my feet. Fire was licking through the ruined doorway beneath a column of black smoke. We hadn't gotten out a moment too soon.

We circled wide around the house and made it to the street. A few neighbors were standing outside their homes, staring at the smoke. In the distance, I heard sirens approaching.

"We should go," Sam muttered.

I nodded my agreement and we returned to Sam's SUV. Adrenaline didn't stop thudding through my veins until after Sam had the vehicle back on the freeway.

He broke the silence by slamming his hand against the steering wheel. "Goddamn it!" he shouted.

"I'm sorry, Sam," I said, my voice still a little hoarse from the smoke. "We'll figure this out."

"How? It's all gone!"

"Nothing is ever truly gone, Sam. They may have destroyed that mural, but those newspapers still exist. We'll find the stories again, no matter how long it takes. We've got more clues to work with now."

"And the men who are following us everywhere we go?"

I grinned at Sam. "You're acting like this is the first time someone's tried to kill you."

"I'm not like you," he muttered, then he sighed. "But you're right. This is what we do."

"How hard could it be? We just have to replicate the life's work of a crazy, obsessed hoarder. Preferably before one of these psychos finally kills you."

"Yeah. Piece of cake," Sam groaned. "What could go wrong?"

THE GHOST AND THE GRAVE

A MAX ABADDON SHORT STORY

JUSTIN S. LESLIE

Story takes place between *The Purity Law* and
newly announced book 3, *The Gate to Everwhere*

HERE WE FIND Max settling in with the realities of the world around him, becoming more relaxed with the Magical and Ethereal communities. The Balance has occurred, and the regular world is now aware that everything that goes bump in the night, for the most part, is real. In this short story, Max, well . . . Max is about to learn a valuable lesson about making bets at the bar with a stranger.

Fate has handed Max something that will affect not only his but the lives of his friends. Only time will tell.

We also meet two new characters that have a rather sorted future in the series. Anyone like pirates and ghosts? There may be a cameo. The Fallen Angel has several ways in from multiple Planes, but only one way out.

Sit back, have a drink, and enjoy the ride.

CHAPTER 1

"Max, can you get that thing to calm down?" Phil said, flooring the accelerator of the Black Beast.

"Trying. I think it just tried to eat my . . . omph," I let out, landing on my back in the bed of the truck.

Phil and I had made the mistake of helping out an old friend instead of going on an all-night bender. Regrets, I have a few . . .

The creature we'd agreed to catch was a rather lively Fiend Hound terrorizing a local beach. Almost identical to the ones we'd encountered in Carvels Manor a few months back.

Coincidentally, we'd kept one of those hounds and given it to Davros, a rather old Vampire that sat on the Supreme Council. Once he'd heard of another one being let loose from the Plane, he just "had to have it."

Shaped like a dog with armor resembling that of a turtle, its massive teeth protruded from jaws sitting below two black oval eyes, all topped off with a tail that could turn one's guts into spaghetti.

"Nah, bruther, I think it's trying to make friends with your leg," Phil bellowed laughing.

While the creatures looked like nightmare fuel, they did have a rather passionate side. Highly illegal, and one of only two I was aware of, we needed to get it off the streets before it caused a scene. Normal folks might not take well to a hellhound running around and all.

The plan had been simple. Go find it (easy part), pick it up (easy part two), and drive it back to the Atheneum. The not-easy part.

I reached down, trying to put the leather rope around its overly wide neck. "Alright, fella, last time. I'm not asking nic—" Again, the beast lurched over, flipping me on my back.

It stood over me, maw open, slime running down its fangs and landing perfectly on my face. The hound's breath was a mix of decay and the ocean. I was guessing it spent most of its day drinking seawater.

I gagged and lifted my finger, pointing a spark of hellfire directly at it, its black bottomless eyes reflecting the blood-red flame. The creature backed up, sitting down in the bed of the truck and lowering its head like a dog that was about to get smacked with a newspaper for peeing on the rug.

"Got him," I yelled as the smell of Phil lighting a cigarette filled the air.

I heard him chuckle as I leaned on the tailgate of the truck, wiping my face off and taking a breath of fresh, humid Florida air.

***

AFTER HEARING PHIL tell the humiliating story of how the evening had gone wrong on the way back, Davros nodded his head, turning to leave. Before he did, though, he stopped, looking back at me.

"Max," the smooth yet authoritative voice came oozing from Davros. "Here, for your troubles." Davros flipped a gold coin in my direction, with me barely catching it. "Drinks on me tonight."

We watched as the Old Vampire walked out the door petting the animal on the head. I could swear he was again making kissy noises at the Hound.

"Bruther, you're on your own tonight," Phil chuffed. "It's late, and I have to run a job in the morning."

I smirked at Phil. This was the first time in forever he was passing on a night of drinking. "You alright?"

"I'm tired, and I promised Jenny I'd be up in the morning." Phil looked suddenly exhausted.

"Get some rest. I'm heading over to the Fallen Angel. Two drinks, Scout's honor."

"Save some gas for tomorrow night. I have more snake oil coming in this week."

Phil's magic snake oil, as we liked to call it, was a cure for all that ailed you. Especially hangovers.

After our encounter with Lilith last year, Petro—my trusted Pixie companion who just happened to be on his honeymoon—and I had decided to move out on our own. Plus, with Tom back, things had started getting crowded around the Atheneum.

Trish, the owner of the Fallen Angel, just happened to own the building where the old Transitions Office used to be before it was shut down. Upstairs was a full two-bedroom apartment. Which, again, just happened to be next door to FA's.

"Maybe. I think Kim might actually go on a date with me tomorrow. Tell everyone I said hello."

I walked down to the Postern gating to my apartment. The Postern was a room with ten gates. To date, I had only worked out three of them. Tom, on the other hand, had figured out two others only to basically lose the keys to them. The Postern was everywhere and nowhere at the same time.

The interesting thing about the move had been its simplicity. Tom had given over most of the furniture once he was no longer presumed dead, including King Arthur's supposed desk. Still didn't believe that one; it wasn't round. He had moved back into his old house, only to leave again on some type of job for the council.

When I had moved to my new apartment, Devin had mysteriously gifted me a door that took me directly into the room just as it had been at the Atheneum. Funny thing was, I could still decide where to walk out of that door. My apartment or the old facility.

Making things even more confusing, Devin—whom I was sure was the Devil—had also gifted me Tom's old lab and bar. I was pretty sure Tom had had no say in the matter. Family, what can I say?

The Postern and lab below the office had in fact just moved with me. I had spent countless days trying to figure out the math behind it fitting between the first and second floors, giving up after a long night of drilling through the floor after Petro and I had dusted off a fifth of rum.

Much like FA's, it was simple. Find two locations in the apartment and bind the gates together. Wanted to get to the Postern? Just open the closet. Need to get to the lab? Go through the door under the stairs. While Tom made it appear like some type of Gate magic, I knew Devin was somehow involved. Ying Sue had even come by with a housewarming gift and had been surprised by the gate work. I, of course, kept the source a secret. Still, I believed she knew.

FA's was similar. Its main location was in St. Augustine, Florida. However, you could get there from several other storefronts in various cities. Since the Balance, though, that had slightly changed. No regulars allowed, meaning nonmagical types. Open the door, pass the ward, and there you are. Trish had suggested that there were doors in other places, but had never expanded.

Walking through the door, the smell of burnt butter and steak mixed together with the tang of copper from the rustic roof made a grin form on my face.

"Trish, nice crowd tonight," I said, walking to the bar and pulling out a seat, taking a minute to ensure I had gotten all the mess off me earlier.

A man sitting at the other side of the bar looked up. He was wearing a long black trench coat, sported lengthy hair, and an almost longer reddish beard. The guy looked scary. His trench coat was scarred and tired looking from years of abuse and God knows what else. His eyes glowed for a second as he stood up and walked out. The man to my other side looked at him with a familiar gaze.

"Ya, it's been interesting, to say the least. A few new faces tonight," Trish said smiling.

As always, she knew just what to hand me. A Vamp Amber, made in Romania by one of the most renowned Vs on earth, Anna Vlad. Her brother, on the other hand . . .

I took a pull, letting the night's excitement drain away. "Ahh," I let out, slapping the gold coin on the bar top. "Think this will cover it?"

Trish looked at the coin, cocking her head slightly. She was getting something from it. I was pretty sure Trish was some type of goddess. "I think you can buy all the drinks you want with that," she exhaled as the man sitting next to me leaned over.

"Nice coin," the low, rustic yet precise voice said.

"Thanks, just got it. Not really sure what it is," I said, not caring that the coin had been sitting on the bar before I put it between my teeth, biting it like they did in the old movies.

The man was dressed in a black outfit with a long coat that flowed almost like a cape and a hood pulled up over his head. The peak of his nose and some tendrils of hair protruded out, his eyes glowing slightly. In most normal places, this would seem odd. Not at FA's.

"Tell you what, friend. What do you say we grab a table and play a little game? I win, you can either give me that coin or run an errand for me. You win, I'll give you this."

The odd man pulled out a silver version of the exact same coin, slapping it on the bar top and again getting Trish's attention. I hadn't seen that expression on her face before.

I finished the rest of my beer in one pull, letting out a belch. "Tell you what; you get the next round of drinks, I'm in."

We stood up, walking over to one of the far tables in the corner. Trish had a few games on the shelf by the fireplace. These weren't cheesy board games, though. Chess- and checkerboards made out of pure silver, older than the games themselves, gleamed on the shelf, more for show than anything else. Tonight, however, they would get a workout.

Trish looked at me, grimacing lightly. I think she wanted the coins.

"No Monopoly, I take it?" I said, breaking the silence from the walk over. The man was taller than I'd expected, and stood up with an odd posture. Not too straight, but more than average. The gait of his walk was slightly off, as if his arms and legs were not moving in sync.

The man didn't respond, only grabbed a solid oak case off the shelf. We both sat down. Trish came over with two more drinks, again giving the man a strange look. Not one to signal me but one of slight confusion. She was trying to figure out who or, for that matter, *what* this person was.

Push came to shove, Amon—the ever-hidden cook in the kitchen— would be there to end the world or something like that.

"Thank you," the man said in a polite, old-fashioned manner to Trish as she walked off.

"Chess. It's been a while," I said, breaking the ice. It was starting to get awkward, and I considered the option to just get up and walk away.

Hell with it. I only had a ten-foot walk, and this was the first mildly interesting person I had met in some time that wasn't trying to have me killed. At least, I hoped not.

"I like this place. It reminds me of home," the man said, pulling the cloak off his head, revealing a full head of immaculately straight hair. He had a serious face, and also one that was not from here, I reflected, trying to pinpoint what he was.

Much like a craft—one of those human husks driven by a Mage or Fae—unless you knew what to look for, one would never spot most of these creatures in passing. People in the know, on the other hand, didn't give it a passing thought to how obvious it was. This man was in that same category. I knew he was not, in fact, human.

"What's your name?" I asked, taking a pull of my beer. A few people had turned around to watch the game getting ready to unfold.

"Penance."

"That's a new one. I thought that was something you did."

"You're smarter than you look. It is. I don't think you could pronounce my real name."

The man opened the chess case, putting down the marble board. Pieces were placed as we both sat in silence. Admittedly, I had forgotten how to set up all the pieces. Penance blew out a huff of air and reached his long feathery fingers across the board to make some adjustments.

"Chess reminds me of life," the man started back up. For some reason, I wasn't really fazed by the oddness of it. "The moves you make in the beginning most definitely affect the ending."

"Well, you just reminded me I need another drink," I said, nodding over at Trish. We had drawn a small crowd around the table.

The lights were dim, the sounds of clinking glasses and low murmurs filling the air.

We looked at each other for a minute before Penance spoke up, "Are you sure you want to play?"

Looking around, I had a feeling the crowd wanted a show.

"Yup, let's do this," I said, giving him the go-ahead for the first move.

He struck out with his left knight, setting the tone for the rest of the match. For twenty minutes, we shuffled pieces while I chewed a light spot on my lip as I watched the cool, calculating player at the other end of the board.

"Checkmate," Penance purred in finality.

I stared at the board, sure I hadn't left an opening. There it was.

Jeers came from the crowd as the man's stare never faltered.

"Best two out of three?" I asked, sizing up the bet.

The man speculated for a minute. "Alright, tell you what. With game one, you owe me a favor. Payable in the next twenty-four hours. Game two is for the coins. I'll even pay you for the trouble of the favor," Penance said, the gold coin weighing heavy in my pocket.

I glanced over at Trish, seeing a neutral look on her face. She wasn't giving anything away tonight.

"Deal," I said as we reset the pieces.

I started this time, leading with my pawns, followed by my knights. The man did the same, mirroring my moves. I started getting frustrated as I counted down the final pieces.

He had me again. I pulled out the gold coin, smacking it on the table. Not too aggressively, but enough to make a point.

"Checkmate," the cool, calculating voice once again purred in finality.

"So, what's this favor?" I asked, figuring I had just gotten into something I probably would regret.

"Ah, the deed."

Chapter 2

Ever realized you truly just messed something up? I stood in my room, looking down at my phone. A full day had passed since losing my bet with Penance. I was guessing that was a fake name, but nonetheless, I owed him a favor besides the coin Davros had given me.

The task was simple. Go to the Old City Cemetery in downtown Jacksonville and retrieve another coin from the tombstone of a soldier's wife simply named Agnes. The soldier also happened to once have been the mayor of Orlando, meaning that Agnes was once an important person. It was an old military tradition to leave coins on the tombstones of those you'd served with. Different denominations meant different types of military relationships. For tonight, I was to acquire a fifty-cent piece.

Penance had even offered to pay for my troubles if I was able to find the coin. He'd stated, "I'm not allowed on hallowed ground," whatever that meant. I knew it meant absolutely nothing with Vamps, so I was guessing he was just crazy. It all seemed like a bunch of bullshit, but I'd made a bet and knew better than to back out. Once retrieved, I would meet the obnoxiously good chess player back at FA's for a drink.

I had talked to Phil about the whole mess, him agreeing that the guy was crazy and that he would meet me at the cemetery if I needed him to. He was down for drinks later, though, no matter the outcome of my evening.

I decided to gate in from the Atheneum, as Riverplace Tower wasn't far from the cemetery and there was a gate nearby. I kept thinking about Kim and her offer for dinner and drinks being pushed off another day.

The walk was a brisk ten-minute stroll. Since the Balance, people were more aware than before. In the past, walking through this part of Jacksonville, Florida would have garnered you a few mean stares. Now, people were more concerned with if you were going to eat them or maybe turn them into a rat. Both just happened to be very rude and way too old fashioned, even by Mage standards.

Arriving at the cemetery gates, a sinking feeling dropped in my stomach like a load of tacos after midnight. Something was hitting my senses on all cylinders. I hadn't felt this much energy since our trip to the South Pole, which had subsequently resulted in the destruction of a rather old geological feature. I had a reputation for that kind of stuff.

The night was humid. Moisture hung in the air as a light breeze ensured it stuck to you. The smell of grass, river water, and garbage from the city filled the air. Looking around, it was clear that the full moon was casting shadows at all angles. It was the perfect night for trouble.

I patted my blazer, ensuring I had all the necessary tools to protect myself. Durundle, my service pistol, and a few blended items, including an Evergate coin, were all in place. As always, the Evergate coin would bring me right back to the Postern and home. For a few minutes, I thought about going back to FA's to get more details from this guy, but figured it wouldn't matter.

There was trouble ahead, and I didn't have a clue what type.

There were a few large ornate grave markers I remembered seeing as a child. The one I was to go to tonight had been made for someone named Agnes, the wife of a former captain and once mayor of Orlando. An angel was represented on the marker, and I was to check there first.

The coin had been left there by James, Agnes's husband, and to date, no one could or had removed it.

I walked up, not noticing the man sitting on the curb holding a small alligator.

The man let out a laughing cackle. "You sure you want to go in there, fella?" he asked in a scratchy, high-pitched tone.

I didn't have to get much closer to see he was more than likely a crackhead. Well, a crackhead with a pet alligator. I could lightly sense something coming from it.

I reached in my pocket, throwing the man a five. "Get something to eat. I'll be fine. Anything I need to know before I go in there?" I asked, figuring he had spent a good amount of his time in that spot.

"Are you afraid of ghosts?" the man cackled back, tucking the money in his pocket.

"I guess a little. Who isn't?" I said, taking that in.

"Sounds like you're smart enough. You'll be fine," the man replied, standing up and holding the small alligator under his arm. "It's OK, Ralph. The dead man's not going to hurt you," the bum said, cooing at the animal before walking off.

I looked at the gate, the moon lighting the treetops. Walking around, I found a gap in the fence and squeezed through, grumbling about having to suck in way too much.

The scene inside the graveyard was textbook. A light fog covered the ground, making it hard to see your shoes. Shadows danced around the gravestones and trees, while the noise of the city in the background contributed odd sounds that were hard to pick out.

The ground was crunchy underfoot; gravel with grass that hadn't been properly maintained.

Unease settled in, convincing me to pull out Durundle. I could still see due to the moonlight, but for some reason, sounds were bouncing off everything. Echoes of voices, cars being driven, and metal clanking on concrete.

I started focusing on one tree in particular. Scratching could be heard, loud, distinct, and absolutely coming from the tree. I walked, stubbing my toes on a few low headstones that had been worn down to nothing but small rocks.

"Shit," I hissed, almost losing my footing, eyes laser focused on the tree. No movement.

Within five feet of the tree, I could finally see what was causing the noise, making the hairs on my neck stand at full attention.

There, on the other side, was a rotted hand, the tip of a finger showing nothing but bone scraping the bark of the tree. It had dug a sizable hole in the trunk. The figure was covered in a dark, tattered robe, its face shielded from sight. Rasping came from the dark void.

"Ignis," I whispered, pushing my will to the blade and springing it to life. Today, the sword had decided it would be a muted blood-red glow, not the flaming sword it was known to be. It had a mind of its own.

The creature didn't flinch as the red glow of the blade lit up what was once a face. Grated meat and bone flickered red as empty eye sockets stared at the tree, determined to keep digging.

The sound stopped. Holding my breath, I took two more steps to the side. It was like the thing didn't know I was there.

I was wrong . . . the now animated creature lurched backward, pointing the sharpened finger it had been digging with at me. Jumping back, I pulled Durundle into the guard position above my head. The creature froze.

No longer in the shade of the tree, I could see the shimmer of moonlight passing through its apparitional body.

"Gods and graves, a ghost? You have to be shitting me," I said, seeing my breath floating in the air, neither one of us moving, both sizing the other up.

For all intents and purposes, this was in fact the first ghost I had run into. Sensing my distraction, the creature lurched again, swiping through the air with a violence to its speed and power that was very real.

If the bag of bones had landed that, I would've been in trouble. Still on my guard, I slashed down with my sword, cutting through the air. The whoosh of the blade sliced through the spirit and caught on what felt like meat and bones.

The ghost solidified under the smoldering of hellfire now burning its cut-in-half body, fingers twitching as fabric disappeared. Looking closer, as the flame had cleared some of the fog, I could see both the creature and hellfire slowly winking out of existence.

Soon, I looked down to see no trace of either.

The familiar cackle of the old disheveled man with the alligator cut through the silence as I stood there, taking it in. "Looks like that one will not be coming back. The second death," the man said, chuffing. The alligator was now walking on a leash at his feet. The sound of him drinking a Slurpee echoed lightly as he hit the bottom of the cup.

"So, that was a ghost," I said, knowing from talking with Tom that they did exist. It's not that I doubted him. I just had never seen one before. "Second death?"

His alligator's tail was wagging like a dog's. "Hellfire is one of the few things that will do it. So, I'm guessing you're not exactly one of those normal magic types. You might just get what you came here for."

I was starting to think the man in front of me was putting on a show.

"What's that?" I asked, putting Durundle back in its sheath.

"The coin. Every once in a while, someone shows up looking for it. They can't even find it or see it. After what you just did, I'm pretty sure that part will be easy," the man replied, again taking a slurping drink through his straw and finalizing the last of his slushy.

"So there's a hard part?"

"Yup. Give me a couple more bucks. I want to go get a refill and watch."

I dropped five more dollars in his hand. The alligator hissed at me as the man giggled, walking off.

Chapter 3

After a few minutes of reflecting and trying to figure if what had just happened had, in fact, just happened, the distant cackle of the odd man ground me back in reality.

"Where did he get that Slurpee?" I huffed, talking to the night air.

I pulled my short staff out, feeling its carvings under my fingers. I wasn't sure if killing ghosts was a good thing or not. I already had sleep issues.

Getting my bearings, I headed deeper into the cemetery noticing more apparitions. Old headstones and unkempt ground crunched under my feet.

The old man with the alligator had stated they couldn't hit me "here," whatever that meant.

I looked over to see a woman sitting on a stone bench. The moonlight shimmering through her body let off a slight glow.

Unlike the creepy skeleton fingering the tree, she looked normal. Sad, but otherwise put together. Her dress reflected early to midcentury fashion. I was guessing the '20s.

I squatted down, getting eye level with her. She reminded me of Leshya. It was something about the eyes, or maybe the stare. Tom and I needed to have a chat about her some time. It was due. After all, he was a necromancer, and what I was looking at was reminding of Leshya a little too much.

The figure slowly looked up at me. She had been crying for what I guessed was decades. The apparition looked straight through me before her eyes finally came into focus, showing confusion.

"Hey," I said in a low voice, seeing if it caught her attention.

The woman stared for a second before looking back down at the grave.

"Something there you need?"

She looked up at that, cocking her head. Like most people, I had watched enough ghost movies to know that usually got one's attention.

Hell, after the Balance, the world had suddenly realized that most movies Hollywood pumped out were moderately instructional after-school specials.

The woman paused again, looking down at the grave. I took a minute to regain my bearings, figuring I would come back later and check it out. Maybe I'd even bring Tom, when he got back from wherever the hell he was.

As usual, not long after he showed up, he disappeared again.

I walked another fifty meters toward the large, carved grave marker. For some reason, more apparitions started showing up the closer I got to my target. I noticed a few taking a keen interest in my movements.

Checking my watch, I noticed Phil hadn't responded. The message was blue, so he had, in fact, gotten it before I left.

The large statue stuck out like a sore thumb even in the dark. It also appeared to have power pouring out of it, raising the hair on the back of my neck.

I looked down, shining the light of my phone on the name and confirming this was Agnes's grave. Inspecting the statue, I noticed the hand of the angel was reaching down to what looked to be Agnes holding a child. No coin.

Coins were convenient vessels for enchantments and spells. The metal carrying the Etherium allowed it to be stored and used to the best of its abilities. I could feel power coming from the shrine, but again, no coin.

Looking closer at the statue, I noticed the hand of the angel was smoother than the rest of the stone. It looked like years of people rubbing the hand for good luck, or whatever superstition this had tied to it.

Taking a deep breath and against my better judgment, I reached out and touched the hand of the angel, pushing my will into the statue.

A loud pop of ozone smacked the air as I fell back, the power from whatever it was I had just triggered flowing over my body like smoke. I stood up after a moment, feeling like I had just been sucked through multiple gates at once: slightly drained and disoriented.

Once up, it was clear that, while I was still in the graveyard, I was absolutely on a different Plane.

The shapes of the apparitions, now solid, started moving, noise coming from their sudden unease. I had a strong feeling that they were not so harmless anymore.

Sounds started filling the once silent night. A constant grinding rumble reverberated in the background. It wasn't the familiar sounds of the city, and at that moment, I realized I wasn't in Kansas—well, Florida—anymore. At least, not the one I knew.

Patting my blazer, I checked that Durundle and my short staff were still there. The hilt brought comfort to my otherwise freaking out mind.

A pirate—I was guessing "pirate" due to his clothes—stood approximately ten feet away. The long, flowing black beard made the scowl on his face more intense and threatening.

He of course, upon further inspection, had a peg leg and an exceptionally large saber in hand.

The look on his face was one of calculation; he had yet to figure out what I was. I was the new fish in the tank, and the pirate was the shark. As I guessed any good pirate would, he decided to attack first and ask questions later.

His saber whistled down. Instinctively, almost as if on cruise control, I pulled Durundle from its sheath, filling the night with glittering red hellfire.

When the sword decided to go into this mode, it made the surrounding area look as if someone had dropped a red flare.

For those not aware, the sword had a mind of its own at times. Moving and pushing me in ways I normally wouldn't be able to accomplish.

The one thing about a trained swordsman or woman was that they had usually done it all their life. I was new to the sword game, and on top of that, my attacker had what looked to be a few centuries of practice.

In most cases, years of experience was the reason Mages were so skillful at using hand-to-hand combat weapons. Decades of practice left even professionals at the top of their game outclassed when compared to Mages. Mages and Ethereals alike often didn't even enchant their weapons as they were, in fact, that good.

I was not at that level yet, so Durundle again came to life, taking on a mind of its own and driving my hands to work on a level I had yet to earn. Hey, if you're not cheating, you're not trying.

The hissing blade swung down, slamming into the saber. It was the first time the sword hadn't eaten through whatever it touched. We both pulled back, reassessing. The large bearded man lunged again, leaving his lower body and peg leg open.

Swinging again, I missed his blade on purpose, instead aiming for the odd-looking wooden leg. The effect was fast and final as the man fell to the ground. A bellow of frustration came from his throat, death shooting from his eyes.

I had attacked not only him but his pride. My thinking behind that was not to kill any more ghosts, sending them to their final death—or under my bed at night.

Walking closer, I saw what I was looking for: a coin just like the one I had hanging off his neck on a chain that fell out when he hit the ground.

We looked at each other as he started crawling toward his saber. A flaming arrow whistled through the air, hissing as it passed my head and cut my cheek. I crouched, looking around.

No origin. The pirate, knowing its invisible source, did as any pirate would and started cussing.

"Hornswoggling, ass jack!" the bearded man on the ground exclaimed in a rough, bellowing voice, his accent not placeable but there. He was not happy with the arrow, directing his curses toward the new attacker.

Great, more issues, I thought, darting around the statue and touching it again in hopes of leaving. Nothing. Another arrow slammed into the statue from behind. Either the attacker was lightning fast or there was more than one.

Other figures once looming also dove for cover. I think I triggered the security system, whatever that is in an old graveyard in another Plane.

Another flaming arrow forced me to my feet and on the move. I ran back in the direction I had come. Maneuvering around trees, the arrows slowed down. The shuffling of feet away from the statue filled the air. Whatever was throwing the flaming arrows had everything else in the cemetery going for cover.

I looked to the right, seeing the familiar outline of the sad woman, now solid, still sitting on the bench. This time, she was pushing a hand into the ground with her feet as she wept. The scene was surreal.

Letting out a light whistle, her strained look of concentration broke for a moment as she looked up. She motioned with her head for me to come over. The look was pleading.

I wasn't sure if my second attacker was bound to a certain area, but decided to take my chances, slowly creeping out from behind the tree.

"Please," the woman said in a breathless voice that had been holding in that very word for decades.

The hand was gnarled, its familiar, pointed fingers sticking up razor sharp. Grayish skin stretched to the point of eruption on the knuckles.

It was the hand of a vampire. Issue was, here, I couldn't figure out if it was dead, alive, or somewhere in between.

The hand looked apparitional, not solid like the other figures, telling me that in the world I had just come from, it was in fact very real. It appeared the woman was trying to keep it from crossing over. Things here were the opposite.

She looked at the sword in my hand. I had let the flames out when I'd gone on the move, seeking concealment.

A flaming sword was probably the most conspicuous thing one could have.

"You want me to," I asked in the form of a statement, referring to driving the blade through the ground into whatever lay beneath.

The woman started shaking as her mouth slowly started moving. She was pretty in an eerie manner, like Leshya.

"Cannot leave. He can't leave," she said in a strained, hushed voice.

I looked back, seeing movement in the shadows but no more arrows.

"Why?" I asked, the look of frustration growing on her face.

"Spread pain, death, sadness," she said, her hushed voice growing slightly louder. The hand was becoming more animated as she spoke, reacting to her voice.

In reality, I was not sure what the repercussions of killing something in this plane could possibly be. I wasn't under immediate threat. The woman obviously was . . .

I couldn't do it. Noise again filled the air, bringing my senses back into focus as the ground under the hand started moving.

A quick snap of wood echoed as the hand reached toward the foot the woman was using to push the vampire down. A moment later, the other hand erupted, grabbing the woman firmly by the ankle.

She gasped as fear crossed her face. "OK, now we have an issue, buddy," I said, igniting Durundle sweeping down on both hands, sending them flying through the air.

The woman gasped, her eyes going wild. She knew death awaited her at those hands.

I swung the sword overhead, holding it upside down as I decided the location to land the hit. Taking a breath, I thrusted down the center of the now gone hands. The sword plunged into the damp earth with no resistance, the flaming blade hissing as it pushed further into the ground.

The two stumps spasmed then fell still.

I looked over to the woman wearing a nervous smile. Not out of happiness but out of mercy, and regret. You know, the smile you saw at a funeral when someone was remembering better days long since past.

She reached toward me as her solid body faded away into mist.

The roar of an engine, followed by two beaming headlights, flooded the cemetery. Figures shuffled out of sight. In the far distance, two long-dead soldiers stared blankly into the light.

There was something unearthly about the entire situation. The sky above had an odd purple hue to it, and the light odor of wet, stale soil filled the air.

As if reading my mind, the black-bearded pirate turned to see the headlights, his eyes gleaming in the sparkling illumination.

The angry pirate was dragging himself toward the monument and grave marker for Agnes . . . I caught his eyes looking up at the trees before turning back to the task at hand. Getting to the monument.

My stomach dropped, thinking of the repercussions. I wasn't an old wise mage, but I knew that the coin on his sash was in fact a gate coin, and the monument was some type of gate. I was betting that if he made it to the monument, I would be stuck.

We both refocused at the same time. I pulled out my service pistol and slammed Durundle into its sheath, the blade disappearing into the enchanted hilt and dissolving its size.

Phil had taught me a thing or two. Mainly that I was better off carrying "loaded" ammunition made specifically to handle Ethereals and Mages.

Taking off at a sprint, it was clear that whatever was slinging arrows or driving the vehicle didn't have the same agenda. Arrows flew overhead, precise and rhythmic. One arrow landed close to my feet, the person behind the flaming bolts letting me know I was next.

The sound of broken glass filled the air as I finally caught up with the bearded man. He had turned and was pointing his saber at me. A look of determined hate filled his face.

I politely pulled up my pistol, pointing it at his face. Again, the sound of an engine revving filled the air, the lights shifting as the arrow-shooting part of the party kept firing at the vehicle.

"So, two options," I said to the pirate, feeling a light hammering on my chest.

"Looks like you have other problems, scallywag," the man said in a deep, rumbling voice.

"No, we have a problem. I saw the arrows skinning your ass as well," I said in a rush, knowing time was ticking.

"Give me the coin, and we will call it even."

"What if I don't," the man said in serious reflection. He was not as ignorant as he looked.

"Then we have a problem that will not end in your favor."

The man let out a laugh as the sound of a vehicle crashing into rock filled the air. Whatever had happened with the other parties in the cemetery was over.

"Here. Before you leave, know that everything you take has a price to it. I'm not giving this to you freely."

Motioning for him to throw the coin, he tossed it at my feet in a sash. He hadn't looked at the pistol once, telling me he didn't see it as a threat. I'd spotted an old flintlock pistol in his waistband earlier.

Something wasn't adding up with the man either way. I wondered for a slight second if he was like me, stuck on this Plane.

The first arrow slammed into the man's shoulder. He didn't move. A smile crossed his face as he pulled out his pistol. I started to squeeze the trigger, and the flintlock pistol roared to life. The round screamed by my ear, filling it with the familiar buzzing ping I had grown to know in the army.

The shot had staggered me, slightly blurring my vision.

The man laughed again, the sound muffled. His mouth was full of black and gold teeth. He started cackling, looking over my shoulder.

The sound of flesh crashing to earth filled the ringing silence. Again, the man laughed. Whatever had shot the arrows at us was no longer a threat. He'd pulled the pistol and shot before I could react. The pirate could have killed me at any time.

Done playing games, I picked up the sash holding the coin in my hand. Power radiated from the piece, flooding my senses.

I pulled the coin out of the cloth and held it to the hand in the monument, willing to leave.

The sounds of laughter filled the air as the familiar pull of a gate dragging me back to reality filled my body.

Unlike with normal gating, I was, needless to say, not really in my body at the time of landing. My body jerked as a hammer-crushing blow fell on my chest.

My eyes snapped open and I gasped for air, as my nose was blocked.

There, hovering over me, was Phil, about to perform mouth-to-mouth resuscitation. The hammering blows on my chest had obviously been chest compressions.

I raised my knee, fully extending my leg and pushing Phil back enough to evade the angry, bearded Irish hipster about to violate my personal space.

"You're alive," Phil bellowed, clenching his fists and raising them to the sky.

I sat there, tasting the familiar tang of tobacco. I think he got a few breaths in. Issue was, I wasn't dead. I'd made my way back.

Looking up and seeing the excitement on Phil's face, I decided to let the moment carry on. He, of course, continued.

"I'll never have to buy my own drinks again. You see that," Phil said, pointing over to the homeless man standing there drinking another Slurpee.

Oddly enough, he was no longer walking his pet alligator. It had been replaced by a thick man with a longer than normal neck wearing a green suit and eating a tin of open sardines. Just when I thought things couldn't get any stranger, they did . . .

"Ya, I owe you one," I said, standing up and dusting myself off. "What's going on here?"

"Bruther, all hell. I show up. This guy's drinking a Slurpee with this . . . well, thing. Next thing I know, I'm running through the cemetery, and a pair of damn vampire hands go flying through the air like whoosh." Phil was good at making sound effects when he was excited.

"Then, I find you lying here stone-cold dead, and then I do my little medical thing and here you are!" Phil finally concluded, lighting up a smoke.

The sound of jaws slapping coming from the man in the green suit caught our attention as he lifted the tin of sardines to his mouth, eating the entire thing, metal and all.

"Who's your friend?" I asked, looking into the reptilian eyes of the now humanoid figure.

"Al. You've already met," the man said, taking a finishing pull from the straw for the second time. I was guessing the now standing alligator had gone from Ralph to Al.

"Fair enough. I think I need a drink," I said, figuring that I had just met my first true shifter.

"Did you get what you were looking for?" the man asked as Al cracked his neck, moving it in a circular motion.

"Ya, you could say that."

"Let me give you some advice,"

Phil interrupted. "Hang on. Do we have a problem?"

"No problem, I can assure you. My companion and I are perfectly fine. Whatever it is you found, take it far from here and never bring it back. Many people have come here looking for it. Most never get up off the ground," the man said, coughing at the group without covering his mouth.

"What's he on about?" Phil asked, cocking his head while still grinning. "Oh, I called Frank to handle the vampire hand thing. Was that you?"

I shook my head, taking the last five-dollar bill out of my pocket before handing it to the man. "Here, the next one's on me," I said as a grin spread across his face.

The two turned, walking off into the fog.

Chapter 4

We both got in the car after Phil gave me two more accounts of him saving my life.

"Tell you what, you've earned it. Let's hop over to FA's for a drink. I'm going to call this whack job and get this mess behind me," I said under my breath.

After a full accounting of events to Phil, I realized he had pulled over and was staring at me.

"What?"

"Bruther, I think you were in the Perdition."

"Perdition?"

"You know, Purgatory, the in-between, whatever the hell else you call it. I've never seen a real ghost, and you just strolled down to the halfway house to hell and picked a fight. I'm not sure about this one; the car saving you, the vampire, the pirate . . . We need to talk to Tom or check you into rehab."

"About that, any word on where he is?" I asked, both chuffing at his joke. Phil, looking concerned, pulled back out onto A1A.

"On some mission. Won't be back for a few weeks."

I needed to talk to Gramps, or as I now called him since his remarkable rising from the dead, Tom. He was, after all, a Necromancer.

Since we now conveniently lived next door to FA's, I took a few minutes to get cleaned up and text the number the guy had left me. I didn't think people really called anyone anymore.

After a few minutes and a quick change of clothes, I received a text letting me know he was there.

This text was followed by a picture of Petro and Macey on their honeymoon. In normal Petro fashion, he was wearing a Speedo while standing by a pool.

There was something about seeing an eight-inch-tall, mustached pixie in a Speedo that made me turn off the screen.

Phil and I talked prior to going into FA's. He was to carry an e-meter in his pocket to see if he could get a reading off the guy. The meter was handy in figuring out what type of person or thing someone was.

We weren't expecting trouble, especially not with Trish and Amon running the bar, but something about the entire episode seemed manufactured, like a setup, and I, as always, wanted to know more.

We walked through the door with our usual nod to Trish. The place was packed full for a Friday night, and the only open spaces were at the knee wall separating the dining and table area from the large bar. The smell of copper, cooking steak, and light smoke filled the air.

Trish had hired a few more people to work the bar and was the first to walk up, handing us our drinks without taking our order. As always, she was right.

"Let me guess. Weird guy in the hood standing at the jukebox playing Whitney Houston songs on repeat?" Trish asked me, already knowing.

"Yup. I want to figure out why he sent me to a haunted graveyard."

"I need to hear this one sometime. No trouble, Max, I mean it," Trish said before walking back to the bar.

We shuffled over to the jukebox after a few reflective pulls of our drinks.

The man was staring transfixed at the machine. It was as if he had never heard this type of music before.

"Hey, I'm here to balance the scales," I said, a term used in the magical community to settle a bet or favor, tapping the man on the shoulder.

The man lowered the hood of his cape, turning around with a slight grin on his face.

"The music is amazing, gentlemen," Penance said, reaching out to shake only my hand.

Phil smirked.

"Let us go take a seat. I will get us another round of drinks. If you have indeed been successful, we have much to celebrate."

We walked over to a corner table, pushing through a loud group of Vs out for a night of fun away from the regulars.

Since the Balance, some things had changed. For starters, FA's had become slightly busier due to folks in the magical community wanting to escape somewhere they could—literally, in some cases—let their hair down.

Vampires, thanks to recent books and love-story movies, had drawn a good amount of the regular population's attention. It seemed they still had trouble understanding that being bitten by a V—unless you were a Fae—would not turn you into a sparkly, eternal vampire. Not to mention most Vs were annoyingly protective of regulars.

There had been a few pop-up specialty restaurants and vampire-themed bars openings. These folks avoided them like the plague. If you met someone claiming to be V at one of those places, they had either been paid to be there or you were, more than likely, being catfished. There were still bad ones out there, they just didn't hang out at bars that sold Vampire Lover T-shirts.

"Let's see it," Penance said, licking his upper lip, eyes gleaming. Phil had a hand in his pocket, obviously trying to get a reading on the e-meter.

I pulled out the coin, wrapped in a napkin, and let it clunk on the table. It spun on its side.

Before the man could pick it up, I slammed my hand down on top of it, gaining some looks of interest from the crowd.

"Not so fast. I was about killed getting this simple task—as you put it—completed. What's so special about this gate coin?" I asked, seeing the frustration in his eyes. I could also notice Trish peering over as I shook my head.

"Gate coin? It's not a gate coin; rather, a key. A key to a special place. It was stolen from me."

It took me a minute to digest what he'd said, taking another pull of my beer. He was telling the truth. At least, as much of it as he wanted.

"So, let me guess. The pirate stole it from you to do what?"

"You met Blackbeard. I was wondering if he was still alive."

"Alive? You mean he wasn't one of those apparitions?"

"Oh, he's very much alive if you saw him, or he would be in the under. What happened to him?"

Figuring I'd hold some cards to my chest, I answered in my best "holding facts back" manner. "I don't truly know."

The man reflected on my statement. "Fine, and your friend there has already let you in on where you were. This key is dangerous and needs to get back to its proper resting place."

I still didn't trust him as I finally lifted my hand, scooting the coin over.

"Thank you. Oh, and for your troubles." Penance reached into his pocket, handing me back the coin I'd lost earlier and the silver one.

"Do make sure you don't spend these in the same place. I would hang on to them for sentimental value."

Great, another riddle. The man stood up as Trish walked over.

"Excuse me. I'm letting you know you are not welcome back here," Trish ordered with complete authority.

The man thinly smiled. "I wasn't planning on it. Good night," Penance said, pulling the cloak back over his head before walking out.

Trish watched with sharp eyes as the man walked through the crowd, leaving. As the door closed behind him, Trish turned to look at us. Three beers had mysteriously appeared in her hands as she sat down.

I again retold the events of the past couple of days, handing Trish the coins.

"These feel off," she announced, placing them back on the table. "When you brought the first one in, I could feel the power coming off it. Now that they're together, it's changed."

"I'm getting the same thing. My gut's telling me this whole thing was on purpose. Like on rails or something. Either way, I'll put these up and dig into them more later."

The three of us agreed, finishing our beers.

Phil pulled out the e-meter. The device was the size of a large cell phone and picked up specific traces of Ethereum. In turn, it would then supply a few readings to help determine how long the traces had been present—not useful here—and the type of Mage/Ethereal or lack thereof.

The meter gave a neutral reading, much like the one it gave when used on me.

We all looked at each other.

"I'm pretty sure he's not a demon," I said, grinning slightly. After all, I was a quarter demon, and had a good feel for the type.

Trish leaned forward to gain more privacy. "I think he may have been one of the Old Gods, or an Ethereal deity of some type."

"Can you translate that, lass," Phil said, rolling an unlit cigarette in his mouth.

"A messenger from the gods, here for a reason," Trish clarified, making ghost noises as she stood up, lightening the mood. "Good night, boys."

We said our good nights, walking the few steps needed to the apartment. I had talked to Phil about moving in, however, he still insisted on staying at the Atheneum.

"Are you stopping by tomorrow?" I asked as Phil activated the gate.

"Wouldn't miss it for the world, bruther," he responded, saluting me as he walked through the gate.

I was alone in the apartment slash new offices of Abaddon & Associates, which just happened to be having its grand opening in the morning.

Walking upstairs and opening the nightstand drawer, I deposited the two coins wrapped in a napkin.

That night, I dreamt of pirates and ghoulish, disembodied vampire hands chasing me around the beer aisle at Publix.

Epilogue

Abaddon & Associates (AA)

Consulting commercial and private. Questions answered.
Re-birthday testing. Council-certified Castor dealer.

See a Consultant for rates.

A Simple Job Is Never Simple

A Straight Outta Fangton short story

C.T. Phipps

Story takes place after book 2, 100 Miles and Vampin'

Chapter 1

I stared at the chess set in front of me. It was a cheap plastic one that was available for about five dollars at your local Walmart. I used to love the game back in high school and had often challenged the old guys who hung around Belle Isle Park to games. I'd almost always gotten my ass kicked, but it'd meant hearing fascinating stories. If you wanted to hear something interesting, you needed to talk to an old guy about living in Detroit during its heyday: civil rights, riots, war stories, Motown, rock and roll, plus the most beautiful cars that ever had existed.

Mind you, that was before I became a vampire. Yeah, after that happened, I wasn't so interested in listening to the stories about old guys. Hell, even before that, I'd served two tours in Iraq, and that had left me with enough stories of my own to tell. Horrors that didn't include werewolves, vampires, vampire hunters, mages, and whatever else occupied my life these days. Still, I had a night off as the bellidix (vampire sheriff) of the now gentrified and casino-fied New Detroit, and somehow that had led me back here. I'd been planning on seeing if any of the late-night joggers were interested in being a snack (I never killed my prey unless they really had it coming) when I'd seen the guy now sitting across from me.

Melvin Johnson. Melvin Johnson was a middle-aged Black man with long hair trailing back from a bald head. He was dressed like it was the 1970s with a purple jacket that opened to a magenta shirt that exposed copious amounts of chest hair. Melvin had been sort of a second-rate Marvin Gaye, and had a distinct resemblance to Bleeding Gums Murphy from the early days of The Simpsons. He was also the singer behind such classics as, "Let's Get Busy" and "Dat Ass." Melvin was most notable for the fact that he'd died in 1982, and I was sure he wasn't a vampire, since he'd been decapitated in a cocaine-fueled car wreck. His presence here in the park, playing chess, had been enough to attract my attention, even if I probably should have known better than to make a wager.

***

"It's simple," Melvin said. "You win and I'll do you a favor. I win, you then do me a favor."

"What kind of favor?" I asked, knowing better than just to take him at his word. "We talking Godfather favor or pick up my laundry favor?"

"Equivalent exchange," Melvin explained. "Equal to the value of an autographed record of mine."

"Pfft," I said. "That's assuming I could even find a record player to play it."

"Vinyl is making a comeback, Peter," Melvin said, reaching over and taking a sip from an old-style Coca-Cola bottle from before they substituted fake sugar for the real deal.

"How did you know my name?" I asked.

"Everyone knows Peter Stone," Melvin replied, chuckling. "The other Black vampire."

"Other Black vampire?" I asked, wondering if he meant my creator Thoth, or any of the other powerful Old Ones I'd encountered over the years.

"Sorry, Peter, but you ain't no William Marshall," Melvin said.

I chuckled, nodding. "I don't mind playing second fiddle to Blacula. I remember seeing that movie when I was seven on VHS. It made me think being undead wouldn't be so bad."

Melvin snorted. "How did that work out for you?"

I thought of all the horrible things I'd witnessed, the people I'd killed, and the beautiful women who'd betrayed me. "Pretty good, actually. It sure as hell beats being human."

Melvin gave an enigmatic smile. "Come on, you know you want to make this bet."

"I really don't," I countered. "My mom was a fan of your stuff, not me."

"Then give it to her," Melvin said.

"She's dead," I replied dryly.

"Then do it in her honor," Melvin continued.

I sighed. "I really do want to get to the bottom of this. Are you a ghost? Shapeshifter? What?"

"Just play the game, Pete," Melvin said.

I pointed at him. "Fine, but I'll have you know I'm quite good at chess."

Just not good enough.

***

"MOTHERSUCKER!" I SNAPPED after Melvin beat me. It hadn't even taken that many moves.

"Haha," Melvin said.

"You knew I was going to lose," I accused, narrowing my eyes.

"Damn straight I did," Melvin gloated. "I am actually a powerful supernatural entity who is just taking the form of Melvin Johnson."

"What kind of supernatural entity?" I asked. "Angel? Demon? Jinn? Fairy Lord? I swear, this is going to bother me all month if you don't tell me."

Melvin shrugged. "I'll tell you when you finish doing this task for me."

I sighed. "That's my life in a nutshell; doing favors for more powerful monsters than myself."

"Life is like a hill made of crap, son," Melvin said, chuckling. "It all rolls down on you until you're on the top. But I'll make you a deal; you do what you owe me, and I'll throw in the record."

I rolled my eyes. "What am I going to do with a gold record?"

"It's valued at about $500,000 dollars," Melvin informed.

I blinked. "You know, you could have opened with that. We didn't need to do this whole 'chess match with Death' thing."

"Who said I'm Death?" Melvin snorted. "Also, it's more fun this way."

I took a completely unnecessary breath. "Okay, what's the object you want me to recover?"

Melvin's eyes became empty of mirth, and his expression turned morbid. "I want you to retrieve the Chalice of Blood."

I stared at him, unable to speak for a moment before finally saying, "The what?"

Melvin blinked. "You're a frigging vampire and you don't know what the Chalice of Blood is?"

"I've been at this thing for just ten years!" I defended myself. "Most of it spent working at a goddamn gas station!"

"A vampire who works at a gas station?" Melvin said, shaking his head. "That's just sad, son. I thought you were the New Detroit sheriff."

"That doesn't pay squat," I replied. "Unless you're crooked."

"I feel like you're missing the point of being a vampire," Melvin said. "However, if you want to know the short version—"

"About time," I interrupted.

Melvin looked irritated. "The Chalice of Blood is the vampire Holy Grail. It's the cup that Lamia drank the blood of Tiamat-Abaddon from to become a vampire. It later fell into Dracula's possession and allowed him to become the second original vampire. Any vampire who drinks of it will gain incredible powers, and it enhances the sorcery of a blood mage to the point that they can work horrifying miracles. Supposedly, it was once used to raise an army of zombies that almost overran New Jersey."

"I think I would have heard of that," I replied.

"Clearly, you've never been to Jersey," Melvin said. "And maybe it was when New Jersey was just inhabited by a bunch of Dutch settlers, but that's beside the point. The point is that I want you to get it for me."

"What are you going to do with it?" I asked. "You need an army of zombies?"

"No," Melvin responded. "I'm trying to save the world."

My eyes widened.

Melvin burst out laughing. "No, actually, it's just a few hundred people. That's enough, though, right?"

I stared at him. "Who has the Chalice of Blood now?"

He told me.

***

"MOTHERSUCKERS," I MUTTERED, staring at the church across the street. "The goddamn Knights of Purity."

It was about five in the afternoon, with the sun not quite having set but no longer in the horizon. We were a few miles outside of Ann Arbor, in a residential district that I wasn't entirely comfortable driving through. I was sitting in the driver's side of a silver SUV I'd rented, and sipping a bottle of artificial blood that did nothing to ease the need for human blood but tasted damn good. I had a pair of sunglasses on to keep away the extra light from my night vision–adjusted eyes, but also because I figured it might help keep people from recognizing me as a vampire. Mind you, I probably shouldn't have been drinking blood, then.

The church, honestly, looked like an oversized Burger King, with a large number of open windows and a fake brick exterior that highlighted it was a relatively new construction. The place was covered in crosses and garlic bundles. If I was a weaker vampire, the place would have sent me screaming, but I was strong enough to stand at least a few hours of sunlight without anything more than irritation, and holy symbols just annoyed me as long as they didn't have faith behind them. Oddly, the Knights of Purity had a lot of faith, but it felt muted compared to other churches I passed. I wasn't religious anymore—being a damned creature of the night, after all—but if I had to guess, then I suspected the Hebrew God wasn't behind a bunch of Nazi vampire hunters.

Yeah, sucking Nazis.

The Knights of Purity were a Christian Identity movement offshoot that held that God had created white humans in the image of himself, while all the other races, which included supernaturals, had been made by Satan. They believed it was their job to kill and subjugate all of them. The only thing that kept them off the FBI's domestic terrorism list—aside from their leaders being donors to certain politicians—was the fact that they, theoretically, were planning to wait for Armageddon to kill all the people who looked like me. Speaking as a Black vampire, I had issues with every bit of their ideology but was especially offended on behalf of my late Baptist mother.

"Nazis. I hate these guys," a voice spoke behind me.

I did a double take and turned to see a man sitting in the back dressed like Silent Bob, complete with short black beard and reversed ball cap. He had longer hair and was wearing sunglasses that told me that he, too, was a daywalking vampire. He also had a bunch of rune-covered rings on his hands, as well as a magician's cane beside him. I recognized him as Arthur Morgan, another vampire from around town.

"I have a bit more reason to hate them than you," I said, frowning.

"I was bisexual in life, and my dad was Jewish," Arthur said. "Suck these guys."

I stared at him. "Fair enough. Did Melvin Johnson recruit you too?"

"The discount Marvin Gaye?" Arthur asked, showing that strange minds thought alike. "No. It was Mark Hamill."

"Alright, I feel cheated," I said. "Young Mark Hamill or old ass sequel Mark?"

"Old Ass," Arthur said. "I don't even like the sequels."

"I gave them a fair chance, but Finn didn't end up with Rey or that Rose chick. They also teased him becoming a Jedi, and that didn't happen either. I've never felt more disappointed with the franchise, and that includes after finding out Liam Neeson was a racist jackass."

"I had the same feeling about the *Mad Max* movies," Arthur said, sighing. "Thank Marduk for Tom Hardy."

I decided Arthur and I were going to be good friends. My mother had warned me about hanging around nerdy white boys growing up. She'd told me they were a bad influence (and was right), but I could always fit in one more at my Dungeons and Dragons table. Arthur and I also had a few friends in common already, hence why I'd recognized him, though our closest was dead. Poor David had been my Blood Servant, a zombie, and had sacrificed his life to save the world from demons. Honestly, I thought it had been a poor trade-off.

Before I could say anything else, a copper-skinned girl with a short bob popped into the passenger's side of my vehicle. She was wearing a Bambi shirt, a bedazzled blue jean jacket twenty years out of fashion, and a pair of ripped blue jeans. The woman also sported a pair of sunglasses, and I was starting to think we looked like extras from a woke remake of *The Blues Brothers.*

"And who the suck are you?" I asked.

"Jane Doe, weredeer," the woman introduced herself, offering her hand. I could hear her heartbeat and knew her to be alive.

"Well, if you don't want to tell me your name . . ." I trailed off, not taking her hand. "Wait, weredeer? That's a thing?"

Jane frowned. "What? Like that's so much more unbelievable than vampires?"

"Yes," I said. "Holy Hell, is Jane Doe your real name?"

Jane stared at me. "Do I make fun of you, Peter Stone? Aren't you the vampire who becomes a corgi?"

"How the hell did you hear about that?" I looked around to see who might have heard before turning to Arthur. I pointed straight at him. "Do not repeat that!"

Arthur just grinned.

"Like you can become something cooler," I said.

Arthur shrugged. "I become a nine-foot-tall bear. I can also appear as any A-list celebrity if I want to get laid. The power of illusion. I don't claim to be the celebrities, but most of my partners don't give a crap."

I made a face and turned back to Jane. "So, I take it you were recruited for this *Ocean's Eleven* heist too?"

"Yep, Carrie Fisher beat me at a game of craps and told me to go kill some monster-hating racists," Jane said. "My Odawa ancestors would approve. So would my Canadian ones."

"Canadians, great warrior people," Arthur said. "You will be a powerful ally."

"I'm not sure what a weredeer can contribute—" I started before pausing. "Wait, did you say Carrie Fisher?"

"Yes," Jane said. "Honestly, she didn't need the bet. If she wants me to kill someone, they're dead."

"Did everyone get a *Star Wars* visitation except me?" I asked. "I wouldn't have objected to Harrison Ford or Billy Dee Williams. Not Donald Glover; he makes me self-conscious even as a vampire."

Jane shrugged. "I don't care. I'm here for the adventure."

"I'm here for the payoff," Arthur said. "One of the original lightsaber props from the 1977 Tunisia set."

"Okay, now I know I'm getting robbed," I muttered.

"Suddenly, I feel the same way," Jane said. "Not that I'm entirely comfortable turning over an ancient demonic magical artifact to an unknown party."

"It keeps it out of the hands of these guys, and I'm all for that," I said, not entirely comfortable with the arrangement I'd made. I didn't feel like I had a choice, though. One of the most fundamental forms of magic was the geas, or oath magic. You made a pledge on a wand or by pricking your finger, then a wizard made sure you meant it. It sounded like a bunch of Harry Potter nonsense, but people had died breaking their pledges to sorcerers. There was also the social stigma of being an oathbreaker among supernaturals that was about as bad as being a pedophile in prison. I wasn't about to back out on this deal even if I wanted to.

"So, does anyone have a plan?" Jane asked.

I looked back at Arthur. "You said you can do illusions?"

Chapter 2

"This is an incredibly stupid plan," Jane said, walking beside me. She now looked like the daughter of the president, with blonde hair, blue eyes, and a plastic smile on her face that made her look like an alien's idea of white people.

"It's working, isn't it?" I said, covered in the illusion of a tall white man in a polo shirt who I think had been based on the preppy kid in *The Goonies*. Arthur may have had the power to make us look like other people, but he didn't seem to be terribly imaginative when it came to designs.

"Unfortunately," Arthur muttered while following behind us. He had his hands clasped together and was repeating a mantra behind us. He hadn't covered himself in an illusion, had just turned his shirt inside out and ditched his dark leather coat, as well as turned around his baseball cap. It made him look a bit more working class, but fully capable of fitting in with the people around us.

Much to our surprise, almost no one questioned us walking into the grounds of the First Church of Purity. They were apparently open to "any and all who sought the Lord"—and fit the appropriate racial profiling. I'd signed the guest book as Bo Duke, while Jane had signed it as Phyllis Schlafly. I was sure no one was actually going to check the book, but it was probably unprofessional on our part to play games on the racists here.

Unprofessional, but fun.

The interior of the church was kind of disturbing with how wholesome and saccharine the place felt. It didn't really come off as the kind of place a bunch of hardcore militant white supremacists were prone to worship in. Most of the people hanging out looked like soccer moms and insurance salesmen. The walls were decorated in little bits of newspaper celebrating members' minor accomplishments, like raising money for a surgery or college graduation. There was even the presence of children's art on the walls. It looked like an ordinary church at first glance, and I was kind of put off that it didn't feel more like a supervillain's lair.

"You okay, man?" I asked, noticing a few glances toward Arthur. He didn't quite fit the perfect yuppie-scum Aryan ideal he was projecting over us. Not that these people were necessarily all cover models themselves.

"I will be if you don't bother me," Arthur muttered between his mantras.

"Sorry," I whispered, not sure where we'd find what we were looking for. "Jane, you getting a vibe?"

"You mean aside from bake sales and privilege?" Jane asked.

"Yes," I sighed. "I'm talking more ancient evil magic."

Jane stomped her foot on the ground and rubbed it against the granite floor. "It's underneath us."

"Underneath us?" I asked. "You sure?"

Jane glared.

"Right, of course you're sure," I muttered, wondering how we would get down. Looking down the hall and seeing an elevator door, I shrugged. It wasn't the most original idea, but we might as well try that. "Let's go that way."

That was when a slightly pudgy middle-aged woman in a long dress and button-down shirt walked up to us. She wore a pair of thick, unattractive glasses that were attached to a chain around her neck. There was something about her that was vaguely sinister despite the fact that she looked like the woman who had constantly complained to my manager when I was working odd jobs in high school. Oh, wait, that was the reason.

"Hello, are you new here?" the woman asked. I saw she had a name tag over her heart that said KAREN.

Of course it did.

"Nope," I answered, looking around and struggling to sound preppy. "Uh, I'm from the Second Church of Purity."

"Second Church? You mean the one in El Paso?" Karen asked.

Jane reached over to the bulletin board beside us and picked a piece of paper off. She even removed the tack. "We're here to listen to Reverend Gordon's speech tonight. We've traveled very far to bathe in his light."

I looked down at her, wondering if she really thought people talked like that here. However, I was out of options. I decided to go full hog. "Yeah, I used to be with the Southern Border Militia, and we illegally nabbed a lot of refugees, but that just kind of pales in comparison to fighting the real evil facing America: them damned dirty commie undead. Especially the Black ones. Blech. They're stealing our women with their unnatural sexiness and edge."

Jane and Arthur both glared at me.

"Excuse me?" Karen asked.

"Fuck it," I said, grabbing both sides of her head and staring into her eyes. "YOU WILL OBEY MY NEXT COMMANDS AND ANSWER ALL OF OUR QUESTIONS."

Karen stared at me, then her eyes glazed over. "Yes, I will."

"Where is the chalice?" I asked.

"What chalice?" Karen said, her voice monotonous and listless.

"You could do this and you didn't tell us?" Jane exclaimed.

"It only works on the weak-minded," I replied.

"Racists!" Jane said.

"I'm not racist, just pro-wh—" Karen started.

"Stop," I cut her off. "Where're the most important stuff here?"

"The hidden basement," Karen answered. "You have to hit the basement button three times."

"You have a secret level?" I asked. "And such a lame security measure? Man, I hope nobody discovers the secret by being testy."

"We've had to kill three," Karen added. "They weren't ready for the cause. Reverend Gordon will begin the Great Work soon."

"What's the Great Work?" I asked, fascinated.

"I don't know the specifics," Karen said. "I . . . no . . . I . . . don't . . . I . . ."

She was resisting the mesmerism, which surprised me. Apparently, Karen was really committed to the reverend.

"We need to move," Arthur urged. "I can't keep this up."

A couple of parishioners passed by and I was briefly nervous, but watched them just walk by. We had to get out of here.

I stared into her eyes again. "Go home, don't speak of this to anyone, and have uncontrollable bowel trouble for the next couple of days."

Jane sniggered.

"Alright," Karen said, blinking. "I'll do that."

Karen proceeded to turn around as I saw myself and Jane briefly flicker to our true forms. I was suddenly a Black man in the middle of a white supremacist church, and panicked at the possibility. Well, not so much panicked as resigned myself to the fact I'd probably have to kill everyone here. Oh, what a shame. No, bad Peter! Human life is sacred! Even these guys! Okay, maybe some of these guys! The kids at least!

No one was in the hall at that exact moment, though, and I guessed we were in the clear. Waiting a couple of seconds, I glared at Arthur. "Nice job with the CGI, LucasArts."

"LucasArts?" Jane asked.

"Not every reference can be a winner," I replied. "What I'm saying is, you can't let our illusion drop for a second!"

Arthur glared at me, repeating his mantra as if to say, "Then maybe you shouldn't be distracting me then, asshole."

Okay, he had a point there. I shook my head and walked to the elevator, opening the door. The three of us piled in, and I hit the button for the basement three times. As the doors were shutting, a tall, muscular blond man who looked like he played college football in Nazi Germany caught them.

"If you don't mind me cutting in," the man said with a mild accent.

I stared at him, unsure if I should try my mesmerism again. It took a lot out of me. I wasn't exactly Dracula in terms of experience with these sorts of powers. In fact, I'd always thought mesmerism was an ability I'd never develop because I considered it so immoral. Free will was sacred, after all. However, life had knocked me around enough to know that taking away someone's choices for a few minutes to an hour was probably better than having to kill them.

"Yes, we do," Jane said, kicking him in the shin and causing him to back away before the doors closed on his shocked face.

The elevator promptly began to descend.

"What the hell, Jane?" I asked.

"We're on a schedule here," Jane said, tapping a nonexistent watch on her wrist. "I don't have time to play nice-nice."

I pinched the bridge of my nose, feeling a stress-induced headache coming on. Funny how those hadn't gone away with being dead. "It's gonna make him suspicious."

"It doesn't matter if we're out of here with the chalice in a few minutes," Jane responded.

That was when the illusion of us as two rich white people dropped, and Arthur stopped his chanting. I was glad to look like myself again, but not terribly happy that Arthur had removed our biggest advantage.

"You outta juice?" I asked, hoping the elevator doors didn't open on an army of Stormtroopers.

"Pretty much," Arthur sighed. "I used to be a lot better at this, but this isn't one of my vampire abilities. It's a psychic one. I maintained it in my transition from life to death, but it's not getting any stronger with age, unlike my other ones. I'm a bit rusty with complex illusions, like multiple people moving through an environment."

"I'll pretend I have any idea of what the hell you just said," I answered, wishing this elevator would hurry the hell up.

"He's like a 7th level Gnome Illusionist, not a 20th," Jane clarified. "Or even 13th."

"Psionicist," Arthur replied. "Much cooler rules."

I narrowed my eyes suspiciously and looked between them. "Are all three of us nerds?"

"I prefer the term geek," Arthur corrected, putting his hand over his chest. "It puts me in a more refined company like Vin Diesel."

Jane gave him a skeptical look. "Uh-huh. You are no Vin Diesel."

Arthur then became the spitting image of *The Fast and the Furious* star. He then sounded exactly like him too. "I can maintain a glamour over myself for hours without even concentrating on it. Even during strenuous physical activity."

I rolled my eyes. Plenty of new vampires seemed overly obsessed with the benefits of superpowers there. "Yeah, we get what you mean."

"Doesn't mean you have it where it counts," Jane said.

"The Bite providing orgasmic bliss to any mortal who receives it compensates for a lot," Arthur responded.

Jane blinked before raising a hand as if to ask a question.

"Guys, can we concentrate?" I interjected. "I never thought in my wildest dreams I would be the serious one in the group."

"I was just going to ask if what he's doing is violating copyright or something," Jane said. "You could be sued for using their image without permission."

"I'm pretty sure it's fair use," Arthur answered, looking like he was treating the question seriously. "Like cosplay."

"You should at least make it a little different," Jane said. "Like Vin Diesel adjacent rather than his exact replica. Hollywood law is rapidly catching up to the supernatural world."

"Just don't ever impersonate any Black guys," I warned, pointing at him. "We have a word for that."

"Never!" Arthur exclaimed, horrified.

With that, thankfully, we finally arrived at the sub-basement, and the doors opened to reveal what was beyond. Which was a basement. I couldn't help but admit to a certain level of disappointment, as the place looked like any other storage room. It was full of wooden crates, spiderwebs, a couple of maps on the wall, piping, and concrete floors. The only illumination was being provided by the lights inside the elevator.

"Huh," Jane said. "I was expecting a bit more supervillain lair with all the buildup."

"Me too," I agreed, frowning.

I stepped out into the basement and the others followed. The doors closed behind us, and we were soon completely in the dark. Vampires had better night vision than human beings, but we still needed a little light to see. We didn't have echolocation or thermal imaging like some movies had depicted us, though I could simulate the former when I was in Man-Bat form—long story.

That was when I reached around on the wall and found a light switch, turning it on. "Thank Marduk for small miracles."

That was when my eyes widened.

"Holy shit," Jane said, looking at one of the open crates I'd missed on my initial entrance. It contained a set of rocket-propelled grenade launchers stacked on top of one another. The other kind of RPG that I had experience with. Beside it was another open box that had about a hundred grenades. A few of them were missing, and I thought back to stories I'd heard of a vampire home exploding outside of Ann Arbor.

Going over to an exceptionally large crate, I ripped its top off and set it to one side. Inside was a stack of FN SCARs, gas-operated self-loading battle rifles. The kind with the rotating bolt. They'd been modified with laser sights for people who couldn't actually aim worth a damn and a thermal optic screen that would allow them to differentiate between vampire and human bodies.

"Mothersucker," I said, looking around for a clipboard and finding one. It listed, plain as day, enough firepower to fight the Biblical Armageddon. Either that or go on a killing spree of New Detroit's vampires and their food supply.

"It appears this particular cult has gone from poseurs to McVeigh in no time flat," Arthur replied. "You don't assemble this kind of firepower unless you intend to use it."

"I dunno, this is America. Still, I haven't seen this much unnecessary firepower since the last time I visited my local police station," Jane added, throwing shade I wish I'd thought of. "They going on a vampire hunt?"

Arthur walked over to one of the maps on the wall and pulled it off. "Not just vampires. This is a map of Bright Falls with homes marked with letters that correspond to a key for shifter types. It lists a few weredeer locations. Isn't Bright Falls the big shifter town?"

"Yes. It's my hometown." Jane looked at Arthur and sucked in her breath. "Sons of bitches."

"Clearly, we have to call the authorities," I said, putting aside the manifest.

Arthur and Jane looked at me.

"Obviously, I'm kidding," I clarified. "We need to blow this place up. Thankfully, I have some training in explosives from my time in the army. We'll pull a fire alarm or something so they can get anyone under the age of eighteen out. Otherwise, let this place burn to the ground."

Both looked relieved.

"Sounds like a plan," Arthur agreed. "But I'm not seeing an unholy grail anywhere."

Jane pointed at the back wall. "There. It's behind there."

Arthur and I exchanged a look before going over to the wall. That was when I stuck my hand out and was surprised to see it pass through.

"I guess we're not the only ones who can do illusions," I commented, walking on through.

Chapter 3

"Well, this was unexpected," I said, staring at what greeted me on the other side of the illusionary wall.

The place was a second church, and not remotely the kind that good God-fearing Protestants would be caught dead in—even racist ones. Nope, not a Black evangelical church. This was more Hammer horror movie with a side order of *Castlevania*. The place was a single large chapel with numerous pews leading down to a stone altar, but that was where the similarities to a typical church ended.

There were black banners hanging from the side of the wall with red, upside-down swords sewn into them making them look like crosses; burning brass pyres sat along the wall despite no visible means of maintaining them, and behind the altar was an enormous goat-headed statue with wings, sitting Buddha style. I vaguely recalled it from Thoth's Tarot cards and thought it was called Baphomet.

Satanism wasn't my thing, and most vampires had less than friendly relationships with demons. In fact, vampires had been instrumental in driving them away from Earth in Ye Ole Days. Earth only needed one alpha predator species, ya know? Sitting on top of the altar, unguarded, was a black chalice that radiated a dark mystical power even I could feel.

"What's it look like?" Arthur called from the other side of the illusionary wall.

"Like Hitler took up architecture and designed the Temple of Doom," I replied. "Honestly, I like it more than the building above."

"You know, I hate that movie. It is so racist," Jane said, walking through. "I expected more from Lucas and Spielberg. You know they had to film it in Sri Lanka because the Indian government thought it was so offensive?"

"I thought it was offensive because of Kate Capshaw's character," Arthur said, following her. "Least favorite of the Indiana Jones women."

"Including the Nazi?" Jane asked.

"Elsa is the perfect hot Nazi scientist. Willing to sleep with the hero and then die horribly later," Arthur said.

Jane stared in horror at Arthur's comment.

I kind of agreed with him. "You know, when I was in the Army, I actually kept the shit-talking to a minimum when I was in a possible live combat situation."

"Were any of these live combat situations in a Satanic temple to Baphomet?" Arthur asked.

I stared at him. "No, I can't say that they were."

"It looks like a Knights Templar facility to me, personally," Arthur replied.

"The guys from the Crusades?" I asked, knowing my military history pretty well. While I'd never gone into officer's training, I'd considered it for a while. Besides, studying previous invasions of the Middle East had seemed like a good idea at the time. Later, I'd met an actual Knights Templar named Renault. He was a self-hating vampire and vampire hunter both. In simple terms, fuck that guy.

Arthur nodded. "Yeah, those guys. What do you know about 'em?"

"I mostly know them from *Kingdom of Heaven*," Jane said. "Mmm, Orlando Bloom."

"The monastic military order accused of Satanism by Philip the Fair in 1307 with the assistance of the pope," I explained. "It was a bogus charge designed to allow them to steal the Knights' vast wealth. Supposedly, the last Grand Master of the Knights Templar, Jacques De Molay, cursed the kings of France so that they would be destroyed within as many generations as it took to reach the French Revolution."

"All correct," Arthur said. "If you had been raised by a secret society of wizards like I was, you'd also know that it was the House that gained the majority of it."

I knew who the House were. They were a defunct bunch of wizards that had previously been the group that had kept the supernatural secret from the world. They'd wanted to wipe out most magical races, but hadn't had the power to do so. In the end, they'd been exposed and destroyed instead. World's smallest violin playing for them.

"Huh," I said. "Well, it looks like someone is either unaware or doesn't care about the whole bogus part of the charges, since this is a definitely real Satanic temple."

"Maybe, maybe not," Jane said, skeptically.

"What do you mean?" I asked.

"There's a lot of magic in the air, but there are no spirits here," Jane explained. "I don't think this place has any real demons here."

"And that's important?" I asked.

"Have you ever fought any real demons?" Jane asked.

"As a matter of fact, I have," I said, remembering the harrowing encounter I'd had with Gog and Magog.

"Then it's a big deal if we have to worry about them," Jane said. "We don't, and that's relieving. Whoever set this up did so to invoke Satanic imagery but without actually channeling the real thing."

"Why would he do that?" I asked.

"Magicians, even hedge magicians, can feed off the prayer of mortals," Jane explained. "If they're praying to a real god or demon, then that energy goes elsewhere. If they're praying to a fake one, then the magician can suck it up to himself. I've had to deal with a few frauds over the years, like the Ultralogists."

"I hate those guys," I muttered. "They've subverted some of my favorite celebrities. I'm ready to break in and rescue Jada and Will if they get converted."

"Thanks for the heads-up, Jane," Arthur said, walking down the center of the aisle. "I say we just get the chalice and get the hell out of here."

About halfway through, the eyes of the statue lit up with a glowing red fairy fire before a horrible booming voice filled the air. "Who dares defile the Temple of Baphomet?! Does thou not know that you are in the presence of evil?"

Arthur stopped and looked back at me.

I blinked and shrugged before turning to Jane. "You feeling a spirit now?"

"Nope," Jane said.

I looked up at the statue. "Is this some Wizard of Oz B.S.?"

"I do not know of which you speak, mortal! Leave now or be cursed and damned forever!"

"No, seriously," I said, walking up the aisle myself. "Is there like an old white guy behind this enormous statue with an intercom? Because I think that would be kind of cool, myself."

"Stand back! You know not what powers you face! I will call forth an army of demons to smite you and bring down the wrath of Lucifer himself!"

"Lucifer hasn't ruled Hell in ages," Arthur informed.

"Do I want to know how you know that?" I asked.

"No," Arthur said.

"Fair enough," I replied before looking back up at the statue. "I'm calling your bluff, Everlasting Know-It-All. Show yourself, wherever the hell you are."

Much to my surprise, a little old man *did* step out of the back of the enormous statue. He looked to be at least in his seventies, might have been older. He was bald on the top of his head and had a little gray hair on the sides of his temples. The man was dressed in a pastor's uniform, and he had a significant stoop in his step.

"Reverend Gordon, I presume?" I asked, making a wild stab in the dark.

"That's Grand Master Robert Gordon of the Knights Templar to you, abomination," the old man said, straightening his back and crossing his arms.

"The Knights Templar died out seven hundred years ago," Arthur said, sneering. "You're no more Templar than I am."

"Not quite," I said. "I've met one of their order. You're one of Renault's people, aren't you?"

Gordon gave a half smile that reminded me of a buzzard looking at prey. "Yes, Brother Renault managed to bring the fire of our order into the Modern Nights before you struck him down, Peter Stone of New Detroit. Abandoned by the Church and abandoned by God, the Knights Templar continued their holy mission of defending humanity against the unnatural for centuries, but we had to turn to alternative means of funding: banking, Protestants, slavery—"

"I've known you like a minute, but I already hate you," I said, interrupting. "Can we cut to the chase?"

Gordon puffed up his chest and sneered. "You've come for the chalice."

"You're damn right we've come for the chalice, you demonic mofo," I said, staring at him. "Mind you, I've come for the breasts of the chalice and am staying for the wings of the planned terrorism. What the hell is going on here?"

"And the winner for most random reference goes to Peter Stone," Jane said. "A Hooters reference, really?"

"It's a fine establishment," I defended. "Excellent food. Especially since I died."

It was always a crap shot to ask the bad guys to explain their plans, but the majority I'd met were narcissistic psychopaths, so there was truth behind Bond villains laying it all out for ya. Still, I was kind of surprised when Gordon started talking. "The Chalice of Blood is one of the many artifacts of our order. It contains the power to enhance the power of blood magic to incredible levels, and will give us the power to cast a terrible curse on the vampires of New Detroit, as well as the abominations of Bright Falls."

"You've used abominations twice," Jane said. "At least give us a different name from vampires: monsters, horrors, nightmares—"

"Silence!" Gordon shouted, grabbing the chalice and lifting it over his head with both hands. "When we send you and your kind into murderous frenzies, it will be the Knights of Purity who put them down. They will rescue the people of this state and be declared heroes throughout the land! The Supernatural Amnesty Act will be overturned, and it will be open season on your kind! The country will burn, and the streets will run red with the blood of the wicked!"

"So, this is a basic Reichstag Fire plot situation," I said, not exactly impressed with his master plan. I mean, it might work, but that was because a good half of the country already hated supernaturals to begin with.

Gordon glared.

"Hey, I'm not the man hanging out with fundamentalist Nazis," I said. "Do any of them actually know how to shoot a gun? Because I want to let you know that even if you give them the best arms, if they're not actual soldiers, then they're not going to look like badass heroes. They'll probably end up shooting each other and civilians until the real authorities arrive."

Gordon didn't look impressed. "You are doomed and will make worthy sacrifices for the avatar."

What a loon.

"Yeah, because human sacrifice is the godly way to do things," I said, chuckling. "Also, no offense, but I'm going to kill you here."

"Are you?" Gordon asked, raising an eyebrow. "I think not."

I looked at him. "Yeah, I'm pretty sure I am."

"No, you're not," Gordon said, lowering his voice.

"What is this, eighth grade?" I asked, frowning. "Time to die, asshole."

"Uh, Peter," Jane spoke behind me. "We have a problem."

I let out an audible sigh. "There's a bunch of evil cultists behind us, aren't there?"

"Yep!" Jane confirmed. "They've also got the armory's weapons, too."

"Marduk dammit," I muttered.

I looked over my shoulder to see half a dozen Army fatigue–wearing men holding the FN SCARs I had left behind me. Their laser sights were all trained on us, and they were led by the same blond-haired Aryan guy who had tried to get into our elevator. Their stances weren't bad but weren't quite up to Army regulation, which made me think they'd been taught by someone who had served but hadn't done so themselves.

A 7th toy soldier—as I thought of them—huffed and puffed as he carried a rocket launcher into the room. He was probably two hundred pounds overweight and had no business in a combat situation barring the invasion of the USA by the Russians à la *Red Dawn*.

"Leave the little bitch girl to me," the blond man said, aiming directly at Jane.

"Someone takes knee kicking personally," Jane replied. "Is it because I'm a woman or because I'm a weredeer?"

"Pick one," the blond man hissed.

"Aw, did your mommy not hug you enough?" Jane asked. "Or too much?"

"Jane, don't taunt the Nazi," I said.

"Why?" Jane asked.

"Because that's my job," I replied. "I've already got a dozen Ken doll jokes."

Arthur was, of all things, praying behind us and repeating a mantra.

"Quiet, Hans," Gordon said. "These three have done us a favor. Knowing what sort of opposition the Vampire Nation is sending after us will allow us an advantage. We have to accelerate the time line of our plans, though."

"You guys really are supervillains; you know that, right?" I asked.

Gordon narrowed his eyes. "Shoot the Black vampire. We still have two sacrifices after he's gone."

That was when the huge statue of Baphomet started to get up, making loud grinding noises as it moved. It let forth an enormous roar that was a dead ringer for the Tyrannosaurus Rex from *Jurassic Park*, too.

"It's alive! Shoot it!" Hans shouted, screaming as he fired repeatedly into the stone statue.

"You idiots!" Gordon screamed, falling to the ground as bullets flew over his head. "It's just an illusion created by the other vampire!"

Gordon was too late to stop the fat Knight of Purity from aiming his rocket launcher at the statue and firing a grenade into it. The resulting explosion slammed into the illusion covering the statue and showered the Satanic church with flaming rock. It also made so much noise that everyone nonhuman was briefly deafened by it.

Perfect.

"Vampire speed, fools!" I said, turning around and moving faster than any human being could in my position.

I proceeded to break the neck of the first Knight of Purity with one smooth gesture before grabbing his battle rifle and unloading its contents into the next one, then another, before clubbing the fat Knight in the face with the rifle butt. It all happened with such a swift, easy motion that I was certain I would take out all seven of them before they could react. Instead, Hans moved every bit as fast as me and pulled out a combat knife before shoving it into me repeatedly.

"You've drunk vampire blood," I muttered, feeling each blow as the knife burned with unnatural power. The knife was orichalcum plated, which was poisonous to my kind.

"Poured into the Chalice of Blood," Hans said, smiling with prominent canines. "I drained two of your kind, and killed their abomination of an infant too."

I stared at him with furious eyes. "I hate people who hurt kids."

Hans slammed me up against the stone wall and prepared to drive his knife into my eye before I delivered the mother of all knees to the balls then tore out his throat with my teeth. Hans screamed, only for me to grab his wrists to hold him tightly. Blood poured from his artery into my mouth like a geyser, and I gulped every little bit down. Hans bled out in seconds, even as I felt his enhanced blood healing in seconds the burning injuries he'd created.

Behind me, the remaining two Knights of Purity were already dead, with Jane holding out a revolver that had gunned both down. Their blood was pouring on the ground and I wanted to lap it up, but I resisted the urge. It just wasn't hygienic, and I was already feeling like I'd eaten six or seven people in a row from devouring Hans. Maybe it was the Chalice of Blood's magic or the vampire blood in his veins, but the stuff was giving me a buzz like you wouldn't believe.

That was when I turned back to Gordon and saw him on the ground, clutching the Chalice of Blood.

"It's over, Father Sardouchebag," I said, making a *Saturday Night Live* joke that like half of my audience would get. Maybe people who'd seen Archer and paid extraordinarily close attention.

"Not quite yet," Gordon said, lifting the chalice after pouring the contents of a flask into it. He then poured the contents down his throat. From there, he dropped the chalice and began turning gray as his body grew to about three times its normal size. His clothes tore apart and he became nothing more than a mountain of muscle.

"Ah, hell," Arthur said. "That's not good."

"It's the Incredible Hulk!" Jane said, lifting her revolver.

I took a thoroughly unnecessary breath. "I take some small comfort in the fact that if I'm going to die, it'll be with a group of fellow nerds."

I then grew a set of claws, stretching out my fingernails and making them as hard as knives, then charged.

Chapter 4

Reverend Gordon had downed some sort of blood cocktail and was now undergoing a transformation into a monster of a type I didn't recognize. The best-case scenario was that he was becoming a third original vampire, and given that Dracula had been powerful enough to become warlord of the entire Vampire Nation within a few years of his transformation, that wasn't a great thing.

By the time I reached him, Gordon was at least twelve feet tall and looked like a gray-skinned gargoyle with a dragon's face. A pair of vestigial bat-like wings were growing out of its back, and a lizard-like tail was coming out of his ass. I know it sounds ridiculous and maybe a little homophobic (vampires don't do homophobia), but he was also waving around his inhuman bait and tackle too. That was just nasty.

"The power of the Elder Gods flows through me!" Gordon said, sounding remarkably like the fake voice he'd put on for Baphomet. "All the nations of the Earth will bow before me. Why worship the God of the Hebrews when they can worship me?!"

"Because you look like a lawn ornament!" I shouted, slashing with my claws into his right leg and tearing into them. The magic inherent to my claws tore strips of flesh from the creature's unnatural armor and caused him to roar in pain.

Jane lifted her revolver and fired repeatedly, the bullets striking the side of the monster's shoulders and chest. The holes created glowed brightly, which told me her gun was magic, but they didn't put down the monster either.

Gordon proceeded to reach down and pick me up in one of his claws, then threw me like a baseball at Jane. Jane turned into a deer before I struck her, bolting out of the way and leaving me to strike the concrete floor with a tremendous thud. I managed to heal the bones broken by this act, but it was already starting to wear down the high I'd gotten from drinking Hans dry.

"Now would be a good time to become a nine-foot-tall bear, Arthur!" I said, crawling to my feet.

"I kind of made that up," Arthur admitted behind me.

"Oh, suck you!" I said, still in man-bat form.

That was when Arthur ran away, running through the illusionary wall. Dammit.

"The Need inside me is beyond anything I have ever experienced," Gordon said, his eyes glowing like coals. "Not just a lust for blood but flesh. I will crunch your bones and tear your muscles from your body. The humans above are nothing now! Merely meat for the grinder! Is this what it is like to be one of the true predators of the night? Yes, I understand now! This is why they look down upon humanity as merely food!"

"I'm pretty sure it's just you," I replied, pouring all the energy I still had into my body as I transformed into an enormous man-bat and flew at Gordon's eyes. I drove my fingernails into them and tore into his face with my feet.

"Argh!" Gordon screamed as he smacked me across the back with his right hand, sending me flying before I crashed down into a set of pews.

"Wait, I have an idea!" Jane said, having resumed her human form.

"What?" I asked, dodging out of the way as Gordon ripped up the stone altar from the church's center and started smashing it down like a club.

"Watch!" Jane said, aiming her pistol at the Chalice of Blood. "See you in hell, buckhole!"

Jane proceeded to fire, and the bullet shot forth and shattered the Chalice of Blood. I stared in shock at the action, which had destroyed the very object we were coming to get. "What the hell did you just do?"

"Imbeciles!" Gordon screamed, dropping the altar and clutching his head with both hands. "That object was irreplaceable!"

"I thought it would get rid of the giant monster!" Jane explained.

"It didn't!" I snapped, wondering if I could risk another attack against the enormous monster.

Arthur proceeded to come back then, holding a second rocket launcher. He had several rockets attached to a bandolier around his chest. He launched the contents of his rocket launcher into Gordon's face, who looked surprised for a second before the front of his face blew off and he fell back on the ground with an enormous thud.

"Victory theme! Da-da-da-da-da-da-da-da! Do-do-do-do-do-do-do-do!" Arthur said, lifting the rocket launcher in the air and doing a little dance.

"Where the hell did you go?" I snapped at him, slowly returning to my normal self.

"To get armed, obviously!" Arthur said. "I wasn't going to leave you behind."

"Thanks, man," I said, genuinely grateful.

"I mean, that thing would have caught up to me eventually," Arthur continued. "It's basic game theory. You get laid more if you help your buddies get laid rather than going at it alone."

I stared at him. "I don't think that's how it works."

"Just thank him!" Jane said.

That was when Gordon screamed and stood up, his face regenerating. "I am going to sucking kill you!" Except he didn't say "sucking."

Jane pulled down one of the banners and temporarily blinded the monster the same way I'd tried. It gave me only seconds to rush back to the dead bodies of the Knights of Purity. Picking up the fat one's launcher, I gestured to Arthur, who tossed me a rocket as he loaded his own. The two of us aimed our weapons simultaneously at his head. This time, Gordon's head was blown clean off, and the monstrous creature's body collapsed for a final time.

I would have fired a couple more rounds into its corpse to make sure it was dead if not for the fact that it melted into an enormous river of blood that splashed over myself, Jane, and Arthur. We ended up all looking like we'd taken the blood bucket challenge. Carrie White would have been proud.

I spit out some of the blood, its taste nasty rather than the orgasmic treat that it usually was. "Well, that was messy."

"The people in the first five rows will get wet," Arthur said, removing his ball cap and shaking it free of gore.

"Well, we saved the world!" Jane commented. "That's worth something, right?"

"New Detroit and Bright Falls," Arthur said. "Not the world."

I walked over to the Chalice of Blood's shattered pieces. "Marduk dammit. How the hell did you destroy this? Shouldn't this thing have been indestructible or something?"

"My gun has an angel in it," Jane explained. "His name is Raguel."

I stared at her.

"What?" Jane asked. "I think it tricked me into destroying it."

"Never trust angels," Arthur said, wiping the blood from his face. "Well, I guess I'm not getting my lightsaber."

I shrugged and picked up the pieces of the chalice. "Well, this is America, and a deal is still a deal. We'll take these to our employer, broken or not."

"My ancestors are Native American," Jane said. "What constitutes a deal in America is a bit different."

"My apologies for all those bogus treaties," Arthur said, heavy on the irony.

"Apology accepted," Jane replied. "I'm glad we can put those centuries of persecution and intolerance behind us."

"Agreed," Arthur said. "What about you?"

"Takes a bit more than an apology on my part," I stated.

"I have Hamilton tickets," Arthur offered. "Community theater version."

"I'll take 'em," I said. "Also, someone to do my dry-cleaning."

"Oh man, it would be cheaper to buy new clothes," Arthur uttered.

"I'll take that too," I said.

"Me too," Jane agreed. "Assuming you have any of those enormous vampire piles of money that I keep hearing about."

"Ha-ha!" I laughed, wishing those existed.

"You got it," Arthur said. "I'll also buy you a car or two. I'm a poor vampire, though, so it'll be a Smart car."

"Oooh, Smart car," Jane said. "Much more energy efficient than my gas-guzzling Hummer."

"Wait, what?" I asked.

Whatever other inane conversation we might have had was interrupted by the return of Karen apparently having gotten over her mesmerism with a minimum of bowel trouble. She ran in carrying a pistol along with a dozen other armed Knights of Purity. These were carrying wooden crosses with the ends sharpened, shotguns, and at least a few machetes. The idea of looting the armory behind them had seemingly not occurred to them.

"These blasphemers have killed Reverend Gordon!" Karen shouted, pointing at us. "Kill them all!"

Arthur looked at me. "Dibs on the secretary."

"Be my guest," I said, staring at them. "I prefer my hunters male."

Jane lifted her pistol.

***

"So, you killed them all?" Melvin asked, sitting across from me in the park. The chess set was set up between us again, but I wasn't stupid enough to challenge him to another game.

"Yep," I confirmed, shrugging. I was wearing a new set of clothes, including a leather jacket and a Detroit Pistons jersey over a pair of black jeans. I also had a leather cap that I felt was suitably stylish. Arthur had been kind enough to help replace my entire wardrobe, and it bothered me that it had all come down to less than two thousand dollars, most of it being from one dress suit he'd bought me for business meetings. Why the hell was it that every vampire in the world seemed to be rich but me?

"Cruel," Melvin said.

"Not really," I denied. "All of 'em were in on the whole terrorist attack. We blew the place up after pulling the fire alarm like we had originally planned. The authorities determined that it was a gas main explosion, probably because they didn't want to acknowledge that a bunch of crazies were stockpiling military grade armament in a—gasp—white neighborhood."

"I'm sensing sarcasm," Melvin said.

"Ya think?" I replied. "Anyway, the Knights of Purity are already suing the State of Michigan for it. I fully expect my tax dollars to be used to help rebuild the evil group within the next few years."

"You pay taxes?" Melvin asked.

"Suck yes, I pay taxes," I said, frowning. "That's how they got Snipes. If they can get Blade, then what chance do I have?"

Melvin snorted. "Grand Master Gordon was one of the last true magicians the Knights Templar still had. He was also charismatic enough to be able to convince people that making offerings to nonexistent demons like Baphomet was a good way to honor God. Without him, the organization will continue to decay and weaken."

"I bet that's what they said when they burned Jacques de Molay," I replied. "If they're recruiting scumbags who want to kill supernaturals, then I bet they won't have any trouble recruiting replacements. The only thing as great as love in this world is hate. At least in my experience."

Melvin gave me a sad frown. "Yes, well, at least they won't be doing it with the Chalice of Blood. You have it?"

"Yeah, but you may not like it," I warned, having come to terms with all of this being for nothing.

I reached into my jacket pocket and pulled out a plastic bag containing the shattered pieces of the chalice. I proceeded to place it in the middle of the chessboard before leaning back and crossing my arms.

Melvin just smiled, emptied out the contents, and waved his left hand over them. Much to my shock and a little bit of horror, I saw the chalice reconstitute itself. It became identical to the black metal thing covered in ancient runes that it had been before Jane had shot it. The evil aura of the object had returned as well, twice as strong.

"Son of a witch," I said, feeling sick.

"It was a mistake to let Tiamat-Abaddon empower mortals with her blood," Melvin said. "It has brought a terrible plague on humankind. No offense."

"None taken," I said, wondering if I should try to grab it and run.

Melvin waved his hand over the chalice and it vanished as if it had never been.

I blinked. "Where did it go?"

"A place where it will never menace anyone ever again," Melvin said.

"Who are you?" I asked, finally getting enough courage to ask.

"God," Melvin answered.

My eyes widened.

Melvin smirked. "Psych."

I flipped him off. "Suck you, man."

Melvin laughed. He then reached over to the side and pulled out a framed gold record before handing it over. "Enjoy your reward. I'll make sure Arthur and Jane get theirs as well."

I reluctantly took it. I probably wouldn't sell it. Well, unless I was about to lose my house or something. "Yeah, I think I'll be going now."

Melvin smirked. "Are you sure I can't interest you in another game?"

Bonus Material

Hunter Blain
Preternatural Chronicles—The Hunted

CT Phipps
Bright Falls Mysteries—Jane versus the Black Knight

Justin Leslie
The Sinking Man series—Sheltered—Chapter 1

THE HUNTED

A SHORT STORY IN THE PRETERNATURAL CHRONICLES

HUNTER BLAIN

Story takes place alongside book 3, *Shadow of a Doubt*

CHAPTER 1

"WHAT DO YOU see?" Ludvig whispered as he crouched behind a fallen log, squinting into the dark. Beside him was his apprentice.

"One, um, troll . . . I think," Magni answered in a hushed tone as he peered through his infrared scope.

"Anyfing behind?" the Swedish supernatural hunter asked.

Magni shifted his focus to behind the troll, making sure his 7.62 round wouldn't go through the creature and hit something else unintentionally.

"Clear," the teenager said in a normal speaking voice.

The troll's large ears pivoted on his Mohawk-covered head in the direction of the duo as he dropped his manwich, the shredded leg thudding wetly on the dried leaves on the ground.

"Fire, now!" Ludvig aggressively whispered with a scowl.

Magni squeezed the trigger, but it didn't budge.

"Safety!" Ludvig chided as a spear whistled through the air. Ludvig exploded to his feet and over the log, catching the wooden projectile between both his gloved hands, the force almost throwing him off his feet. He crushed the wood between his clenched fists before throwing the weapon to the ground and shooting his gaze to where the troll had been.

"Where is he?" Ludvig asked his apprentice, all pretense of secrecy vanishing like a popping soap bubble.

"I-I-I don't know!" Magni stammered in a voice that was losing its cool as he swept the muzzle all around.

Ludvig pulled his rune-covered cold-iron katana from the sheath on his back as he stepped forward, showing himself as a prime target for the rogue troll.

Another spear sailed through the darkness. Ludvig moved with graceful speed and deflected the weapon with the flat edge of his sword, sending it clattering to the ground. He had expected as much.

What he hadn't expected, however, was a fireball with an ice center to be flung by the troll. As Ludvig went to deflect the attack, the solid center exploded upon contact with his blade, sending jagged shards of ice into the Swede's face.

"AH!" Ludvig cried out as he dropped to one knee while rubbing his face vigorously with leather-covered fingers. His other hand held up the cold-iron katana in a defensive stance.

"Lude!" Magni yelled as something crashed into the chest of the large man, sending him tumbling backward for several yards.

Muttering a quick healing spell, Ludvig—the paladin-mage hybrid—restored his sight. Looking down, he saw a hollowed-out log had been thrown at his chest. A quick probe of his fingers determined that no bones had been broken, but his sword had been lost in the tumble.

Magni began firing the bolt-action sniper rifle while letting out a high-pitched cry.

"Magni!" Ludvig cried as he leaped to his feet and began sprinting back toward his apprentice. Passing by several dense trees, Ludvig could see the troll easily dancing out of the way of the gun, drawing closer with each step.

Skidding to a halt while pulling out his rune-covered wand, Ludvig cried out, "Drop!"

Just as practiced, Magni stopped what he was doing and dropped to the ground in a controlled sprawl.

The troll's eyes shot to Ludvig as the supernatural hunter's wand began to glow with energy. With a smile of challenge—which seemed difficult to do with giant tusks protruding from his bottom lip toward his cheeks—the troll's hands began pulsating with unseen power. The air wavered around his outstretched fingers as Ludvig lunged forward, letting loose a ferocious scream and sending an arc of electricity rocketing from the tip of his wand.

The troll's smile dropped into a scowl of confusion and disbelief as the lightning smashed into his torso, sending him careening backward through the woods. A large tree offered some assistance as it caught the twitching body of the troll, unfortunately shattering bones like kindling for the fire.

Ludvig dropped the attack but maintained his offensive stance, wand pointed toward the threat.

"Clear," Ludvig called out, signaling to his apprentice that the immediate danger was over.

As Magni got to his feet, he sighted his sniper rifle and both hunters began tentatively making their way to where the troll remained affixed to the thick tree like an ornament. Blackened skin sizzled as the stomach-churning aroma of burnt flesh wafted through the air. The troll's Mohawk had been singed off.

Magni lowered his weapon as he saw the aftermath of Ludvig's elemental attack.

"Stay on target," Ludvig commanded as he slowly approached the smoking corpse, stopping to retrieve his sword from the ground.

"Why? He's de—"

Bleeding eyes shot open and a blast of energy went out in a sphere around the troll, knocking Magni onto his back as if he had been struck by a three-hundred-pound lineman. Ludvig had anticipated the attack, and dissipated the energy with a swipe of the cold-iron katana. He could have prevented the energy burst and saved Magni from a bruised ass, but thought it an important lesson to be learned.

The rogue supe began to wriggle, trying to free his body from where he had made a troll-sized impression in the tree. Bones began to audibly heal as the skin ceased smoking. Ludvig had anticipated this, knowing full well that trolls were closer to the top of the ladder in terms of healing.

Ludvig placed the edge of the blade against the dangerous creature's neck, and paused.

"Magni, to your feet," Ludvig commanded as he took a step away from the confused troll, who began writhing with renewed vigor.

Doing as commanded, the apprentice first rolled to his stomach before pushing himself up to his feet with a groan.

"Hurry, apprentice. You don't have long."

Magni's eyes shot to his master in bewilderment as Ludvig waved a hand toward the weakened troll.

"Trolls heal quickly. Finish him, now."

The teenager looked between the target and his master like an anxious pendulum.

A hand popped free of the wood, followed closely by a foot.

"Wha-what do I do?"

"Kill him."

"With what?"

"Dat is for you to decide, apprentice."

Another hand was freed, and the troll fell to his knees on the ground.

"Might I suggest you decide quickly?"

"Ahhhh," Magni answered while frantically patting his pockets and tactical belt.

"Use your knife or wand, please," Ludvig instructed as he took a slow, meaningful step to the outside of the triangle the three had created. Ludvig firmly believed in learning things by firsthand experience.

Reaching to the holster on his thigh, Magni pulled out a Glock chambered in 9mm rounds that had iron resin at their cores. He pressed the muzzle of the weapon against the forehead of the troll, who responded by backhanding the weapon with a blurred swipe before crashing his other fist into the bulletproof vest of the teenager. Ludvig tutted as Magni was thrown several steps backward to, once again, land on his inexperienced ass.

"Dey only do dat crap in de movies, Magni," Ludvig chided as he sheathed the sword and crossed his massive arms over the acreage of his chest, still holding the primed wand in one hand. His black leather trench coat flapped in a rogue cool breeze that made the hairs on his neck stand on end.

In elegant answer to his master's enlightenment, Magni coughed out near-airless wheezes as he mentally begged his lungs to fill with oxygen, promising he would never take advantage of being able to breathe again.

The troll got to unsteady feet and started waving glowing hands in the air while facing the teenager.

With barely a tenth of the power he had used before, Ludvig pointed the wand at the troll's legs and sent a fork of electricity into the lean thigh. The troll's hands stopped waving as his body convulsed, dropping him to the ground as if he were a stiff board.

Something in the air demanded Ludvig's attention as a harsh, cold breeze caressed what little skin was exposed, ruffling his soft leather hat and black leather trench coat again. Some had described him as a Van Helsing wannabe, and he was just fine with that.

There was a change in the air, something barely perceptible but there nonetheless. Ludvig's experienced senses sent up red flags in warning.

Pulling out his own Glock from the holster on his leg, Ludvig sent a round into the skull of the troll on the ground, who twitched once before letting out a long, slow breath.

With air finally filling his lungs, Magni's expression soured as he turned to regard his master, who was lifting his red goggles and breathing apparatus into place, completely obscuring his face. This frightened Magni, who knew that Ludvig was now utterly in Hunter mode, and he scrambled on the ground to try and locate his fallen sidearm.

Placing his wand back into his long black coat's pocket and holstering his Glock, Ludvig tugged at a leather strap around his chest and pulled a massive elephant gun from behind his back. The custom ammunition would punch a hole in even the biggest of ogres or demons that were stupid enough to cross his path, or be unlucky enough to gain his attention and become the Hunter's prey.

Finding the discarded Glock, Magni picked up the weapon with trembling hands and rushed to stand a few paces behind his master, scanning the area from his three to his nine as he had been taught. Shallow breaths and a thudding heart filled the teenager's auditory universe, allowing naught in terms of locating the threat that his master had sensed.

"Wha-wha-what do you se-sense, Ludvig?" Magni stammered as he scanned the area around him. When he didn't receive an answer, the apprentice turned to see that he was standing alone in the woods. A tiny gasp of dread escaped his lips as his arms dropped the weapon down to his side, no longer receiving signals from a panicking brain.

A single figure stood about thirty paces in front of the teenager, and the world around him seemed to condense down to a pinprick as paralyzing fear boiled over in his mind.

The figure, clad all in white, approached steadily, confidently, like the CEO of a corporation walking into a board meeting with positive news of growth. Footsteps crunched on the foliage beneath shiny shoes that glinted in the moonlight.

"ST-STOP!" Magni cried out between breaths as he hefted the Glock to shakily aim at the approaching man wearing an expensive-looking business attire. Magni didn't know much about suits, but he had seen enough James Bond movies to know this guy was probably rich.

He was beautiful, with eyes of golden wheat and curls atop his head the same color. His hair seemed to glow as if perpetually cast in sunlight, even though it was the dead of night. He wore a white suit with matching leather shoes and a button-up dress shirt that was only done halfway up, exposing a smooth, lean chest. Magni noticed as the man walked that he didn't have socks on. The smile that decorated his face was alarmingly disarming. Magni lowered the weapon even though a part of his brain commanded that he squeezed the trigger until the weapon clicked empty.

When the beautiful man was only a few steps away from Magni, an ear-splitting explosion sounded, causing the teenager to jump back and shriek in alarm.

Something smashed into the beautiful man before thudding to the ground. The man's smile never faded as he looked down at the silver slug that could have gone through an entire elephant. Magni took note that not even his suit had the slightest blemish.

"I assure you, that is not necessary, Ludvig Mansson," the beautiful man said, never losing his charming smile as he turned his head in the general direction of the blast.

Ludvig came from around a tree with his weapon still at the ready. Magni knew it could fire three rounds before needing to be reloaded. The red goggles never left the man in white as Ludvig kept sidestepping toward Magni.

"How are you—"

"Not dead?" the man finished. "Simple, my dear supernatural hunter. I am an angel, and silver does not wound my brothers or me." As he finished, impressive wings clad in thick, white feathers emerged from his back to flex in a twenty-foot span.

Magni's jaw dropped open as tears of existential awe filled his eyes. Ludvig, on the other hand, kept his rifle trained on the stranger.

"What do you want?" Ludvig asked through his respirator.

"I have come to help you in your mission to rid the world of undesirables amidst the supernatural community."

Ludvig answered with silence as he made it to where Magni was now on his knees, staring with unfocused eyes at the angel. The master stepped in front of his apprentice, breaking his line of sight.

"We have a common enemy, you and I. And I would simply like to help point you in the right direction to remove three nasty werewolves from the Earthen plane. Would you, perhaps, be interested in doing just that?"

Ludvig once again didn't answer, choosing to let the angel reveal more by baiting him with wordless responses.

"I completely understand, and even appreciate, your trepidation, dear Ludvig. However, if I were not an angel, would I have been able to survive the silver slug ejected from your powerful weapon? Hmm?" the angel asked while gesturing with his chin toward the muzzle of the custom elephant gun that was still pointed at him.

Ludvig lowered the weapon, not in a show of affirmation but because he knew the weapon would be useless against this unknown being.

"How about this, then. I give you the information that I have, and you can choose what to do with it. I ask nothing in return, only that you do what you were already going to, had I not intervened."

Ludvig stood a little straighter in a gesture that said he was willing to at least listen while letting his weapon return to his back, freeing his hands.

"Excellent," the man in white exclaimed excitedly while clapping his hands together. "In Houston, Texas, there are three werewolves that have been terrorizing the mortals there, and the Council is refusing to do anything about it, given that most of the supernatural community has, unfortunately, vanished from the face of the Earth."

"I don't suppose you know anyfing about dat?" Ludvig inquired, tugging on his fishing line.

"I am truly sorry to disappoint, as I am unaware of the reasoning for the exodus committed by supernaturals of this plane."

"Tell me more about dese wolves, den," Ludvig said, sensing he wasn't going to get anything more from the man than what he wanted to give.

"Depweg is the pack leader, with his subordinates, Dawson and Joey. They are twins."

"I fink I've heard of dese weres before. Tell me," Ludvig began as he crossed his arms and lifted his chin in doubt, "why is an angel asking me to hunt dem now?"

"I wouldn't ask you to blindly trust a stranger. Turn on the news and see for yourself," the man answered with his award-winning smile and hair and eyes that all but glowed in the dark. "All I ask is if you deem them a threat, you simply do what you do. The world has suffered far too much at the hands of rogue creatures, wouldn't you agree?"

"Hmph," Ludvig said as his chest heaved with the sound. Letting his arms drop, he placed his thick, gloved hands on his hips while shifting his weight to one foot.

"You still do not trust me," the angel said in a statement rather than as a question.

"You don't live as long as I have wiffout a doubting mindset."

"Fair enough. A gift, then, as a token of my appreciation."

"I don't want anyfing from you," Ludvig stated coldly.

"Oh, but you do. Collin," the angel called out to the boy behind the large Swede.

"His name is Magni," Ludvig corrected with squinting eyes.

"Very well, my apologies," the angel said with hands outstretched in placation and a slight bow. "Magni, would you like to know where you can find John Cook?"

Ludvig's squinting eyes violently morphed into a scowl as he bared his teeth beneath the cover of his mask. He was aware that Magni had gotten to his feet at the mention of the vampire and was stepping to stand next to his master.

"Magni—" Ludvig began.

"No, I want to hear him," Magni said with a finality that Ludvig had never heard before. He had always known there was an ocean of strength hidden beneath the glass top of pain and self-doubt.

Ludvig's red goggles smoothly traveled from Magni back to the man in white, indicating for him to go on, for the being had won this round. The Swede knew he wouldn't be able to backtrack without making himself look like the bad guy.

"Take care of the wolves, and I will tell you where—and more importantly—when he will be."

"I thought he was dead or something. No one has seen or heard from him in nearly nine years," Magni challenged, but with a tone that wanted desperately to be disproved.

"That's why the when is so important. So," he turned his gaze back to Ludvig, and the Swede noticed how the smile had changed into a sharklike grin, "we have a deal then?" The man in white extended his hand and Ludvig looked down at it.

Knowing he had been beaten, Ludvig grabbed the man's hand and shook, hard. The angel paid it no mind, as if the man who weighed nearly two hundred and eighty pounds of muscle was nothing more than a small child grasping their parent's hand. This further unnerved the Swede, who dropped his grip and resumed crossing his arms over his chest.

"Excellent. Travel to Houston and remove the wolves from the board. I will be in touch once it is done," the angel said before white wings sprouted again and he rocketed into the night sky with a single flap.

Leaves flew all around the duo as if blown by a tornado, prompting Ludvig to grab the drawstring under his fluttering leather hat tightly.

"What was that about?" Magni asked Ludvig, who was staring into the sky with his expressionless red goggles.

"Not here," the man whispered in answer as he turned and strode to the lifeless body of the supe that had broken the rules.

Pulling out his wand, he waved it over the corpse, the runes glowing. The troll began to rise off the ground, arms and legs dangling, as a sphere of fire burst to life, encapsulating the body. While it was in midair, Ludvig compressed the roiling flames of the sphere until it was the size of a grain of rice, forever erasing any evidence that the troll had existed.

The grain of fire winked out, and Ludvig replaced his wand before taking powerful strides toward the van they had parked on a nearby road.

"Retrieve your weapons," Ludvig commanded with a stern voice as he marched, not bothering to face his apprentice who had unknowingly thrown him into a most uncomfortable situation.

Doing as commanded, Magni holstered his Glock and retrieved the sniper rifle before running to catch up to his master. His foot caught on an exposed root, and he almost tumbled to the ground before catching himself.

Back at the road, Magni replaced the weapon in the back of the van before looking at the car parked nearby. They had used it to locate the troll, finding blood inside and broken glass throughout.

"What about that? Won't the police find it?"

"Get in," Ludvig barked, losing control over his patience.

Magni swallowed as he did as commanded.

Once inside, Ludvig removed his hat and set it on the middle of the dash before lowering his goggles and breathing apparatus around his neck. Fierce, deep blue eyes regarded the teenager.

"Wh-what?" Magni asked with a dry mouth.

"Dat wasn't an angel, boy."

"Ho-how do you know?"

"Foolish child, blinded by revenge," Ludvig drawled while shaking his head and starting the electric van. It came to life, and the Swede pulled out onto the country road in the direction of home, which was about an hour southwest of Houston.

Magni, unable to control his frustration anymore, let rage build in his core, flushing his face and making his skin crawl. "Of course I want revenge on that asshole vampire! He fucking killed my mom! An-and almost got me! If it weren't for Raziel . . ."

"Dat's what you should focus on, apprentice. Dere is good in de world."

"THE WORLD WOULD BE GOOD WITHOUT JOHN COOK IN IT!" Magni screamed, surprising both the occupants of the van. Realizing his transgression against the one who had adopted him and was training him to protect the world, Magni backtracked. "I'm sorry."

Ludvig took a deep breath before turning to look at the teenager he was guiding and said, "If it's revenge you seek, den you must be ready to dig two graves. Do you understand?"

Magni looked at him, trying to decipher what he was saying.

"No, I don't understand," Magni answered in defeat while dramatically crossing his arms and making a show of looking out his window.

They rode in silence for thirty minutes before Ludvig decided Magni had wallowed in self-pity long enough. The truth was, the Swede had needed time to process the events of the night himself.

"Pull out your phone and see what de news say."

Magni turned to look at Ludvig, not wanting to follow orders out of prideful defiance. Ludvig sensed this and turned with eyes that promised it would be a mistake to defy him. "Now," he ordered harshly.

With an annoyed sigh, Magni pulled out his phone, which had been on *do not disturb* while hunting, and pulled up Google.

"What am I searching for?" he asked with a sigh while looking out his window again, frustrated at losing the battle of the wills.

"Search any maulings widin and around Houston."

Magni did as asked, and was actually surprised to see the first article had a title he would have sworn was clickbait.

"*Neighborhood terrorized by pack of wild dogs, leaving several families dead*," Magni read aloud before clicking the article. He began reading it to himself.

"Out loud, please," Ludvig instructed, letting his tone return to normal at the revelation. Magni did as ordered.

Once finished, the teenager closed his phone, and the pair stared out the windshield in silence.

"Somefing doesn't feel right."

"What? Sounds like we got three werewolves that need to be put down."

"Hmph," Ludvig said in answer as his mind considered all angles.

After a few more minutes of riding in silence, Magni asked, "So? What are we gonna do?"

"Follow de lead, for now. Let's catch dem alive. I want to talk to Depweg."

"Um, why? We should just bust a cap in them," the teenager said as he pulled his sidearm from its holster and pointed it out the windshield while squinting down the sight.

"Put dat away. You know de rules about weapons. Do it again and no more movies."

"Ever?"

"Ever."

Holstering the weapon with a pouting face, Magni asked his question again, "Why do you want to talk to, um, what's his name? Depwag?"

"Depweg," Ludvig corrected. He tried to formulate a response as to why he wanted to converse with the wolf, but was unable to. He had taught his apprentice it was best to kill from afar and that it was almost never worth the risk to catch a supe alive, as he had been attempting to demonstrate tonight before the golden-haired man had showed up.

They rode in silence the rest of the way as Ludvig took a mental step back from the chessboard and reviewed all the angles.

CHAPTER 2

Once back at their cabin in the woods, Ludvig retreated to his room and forcibly shut the door, leaving Magni to pause midstep.

The teenager, shrugging off his master's peculiar behavior, plopped down on the couch and turned on the TV, only to be hit with more horrific views about the maulings.

Magni leaned forward on the couch, resting his elbows on his knees while rubbing his hands together. His mouth salivated as a leg bounced up and down repeatedly, unable to remain still at the prospect of the reward that had been offered. Catching these wolves would mean acquiring the location of the murdering bastard, John Cook.

* * *

EVERYTHING WENT STILL as Magni retreated into the theater of his mind and watched from his vantage point inside the car as something tackled his mom in front of his father's headstone. Magni—whose name had been Collin before Ludvig had adopted him—watched in disassociated horror as his mother's skin became pale and sunken within a mere few seconds, like she had been mummified. The monster pulled back a maw bearing twin fangs that poured gore and vascular tissue from between quivering lips.

Then he saw Collin, who was still young enough to require a booster seat, and leaped, clearing the distance to slam into the vehicle. The door was ripped off with a deafening squeal of metal as the beast began reaching into the back seat. Collin, who had been playing with his Avengers action figures, held up Captain America in a defensive gesture, praying that he would protect him from the real monster that was reaching into the back seat. The glowing red eyes still woke him up most nights in a cold sweat accompanied by warm urine.

Only Raziel, his guardian angel, had saved Collin from the snarling beast.

* * *

"RAZIEL . . ." MAGNI BREATHED out as he began sobbing into his hands, trying to stay quiet so that his master wouldn't hear.

A hand rested on Magni's shoulder and he looked up with soaking, red-rimmed eyes to see the understanding look of Ludvig Mansson, the fiercest supernatural hunter the world had ever seen.

Sitting down on the couch near the teenager, Ludvig saw the scared boy at the orphanage whose fanciful story no one had believed. Ludvig believed.

In a fatherly tone, Ludvig asked, "Do you know why I wanted to change your name to Magni?"

Sniffling, the teenager looked up at his master and shook his head.

"Collin was a poor, defenseless boy dat was almost killed by a vampyr in a blood rage. Magni is de name of one of T'or's sons. Do you know who T'or is?"

Magni nodded almost excitedly in affirmation, thinking immediately of Chris Hemsworth bashing bad guys with his mighty hammer.

Ludvig caught on to this fact and smiled to himself as he nodded, not feeling the need to correct the boy. As long as he knew Thor was someone of power and righteousness, that's all that mattered.

"T'or is strong, yes?"

Another nod of agreement.

"Well, his sons are also very strong. I chose to name you Magni because I know how strong you are, inside." He tapped a thick finger against the teenager's relatively small chest. Then again, compared to Ludvig, most people were small. Ludvig had removed his tactical gear and was wearing a black cotton shirt and sweatpants now that they were home.

"I don't feel strong," Magni said with barely enough force as to be considered a mere exhalation of syllables. He began stripping off his holster and body armor, setting them gently on the coffee table.

"You will be," Ludvig beamed with a smile that the boy could feel.

"I want him to die," Magni growled, all of a sudden finding the strength to speak.

"Dere will come a day when you are given de choice between taking a life or sparing it. Dat day will define who you are as a man."

"But he deserves it!" Magni countered, feeling his face flush.

"What did Raziel tell you about John?" Ludvig asked. It was more of a reminder than a question, as they both knew the answer. It had been discussed in great length between the two, as Ludvig had also wanted to know more about this vampire who used his abilities for good. Meeting Magni when he was just a boy and hearing his horrific story had painted a picture of an evil bloodsucker that was hard to erase from the Hunter's mind.

"I don't care that it was an accident! I don't care if he wasn't in control! He," tears began streaming down his red face, "he *killed* my mommy!"

Ludvig wrapped a hand the size of a lunch box around his apprentice's head and pulled him into his thick chest, stroking his hair.

"I know, Magni," Ludvig said as a thought came to him; a test. Pulling the teenager away so he could look him in the eyes, the Swede asked, "If John was hiding in an apartment building and you knew you could never find him again but you really wanted him to pay, how far would you go?"

"What? I-I don't understand," Magni said with a screwed-up face as he wiped his nose with the sleeve of his jacket.

"You have two options, apprentice. De first is to walk away, knowing you will never get de revenge you seek."

"And the second?" Magni asked, indicating to Ludvig all he needed to know.

With a sigh, Ludvig added, "De second is to burn down de building, killing everyone inside."

Ludvig took note that the boy was strongly considering the second option without even flinching at the potential loss of life.

"Magni," Ludvig started after a few moments of silence, drawing in a deep, contemplative breath, "I have heard dat if John Cook dies, Ragnarök begins."

"Like that Thor movie with the Hulk? That wasn't so bad."

Ludvig shot to his feet, startling the boy. Fiery eyes regarded the teenager as a scowl deeper than the Mariana Trench crossed his forehead.

"Boy, stop finking about de movies! Dis is *real*. Are you willing to kill every man, woman, and child on dis Earth in order to get revenge?!" Ludvig boomed. "Fink about your moder. You want dat to happen to everyone? What would she say to you now?"

Magni stared at him with hate-filled eyes before the Swede's words sunk in. Leaning back in the couch, Magni crossed his arms and looked out the back window to the woods beyond.

"Look at me," Ludvig instructed in a softer tone, knowing he had reached the child.

Magni blinked away angry tears while curling his lips before turning to look at the man before him.

"Dat man we saw was not an angel. I don't know what he was, but he knows we can kill John, and even have reason to," he admitted while gesturing with a hand toward Magni.

"Why?" Magni asked with a softening tone and facial features.

"I'm not sure. Dose wolves might be working wif him and be part of a trap for us. Or dey might be innocent," Ludvig admitted with uncertainty, trailing off at the end.

"How do we find out?"

"Only one way to know. Get some rest. Tomorrow we plan. Tomorrow night, we will trap de wolves."

CHAPTER 3

"It looks like they are moving in a pattern," Magni informed from around a spoonful of healthy bran cereal. He made a face at the bland taste that reminded him of cardboard. The teenager longed for a spoonful of sugar, maybe even an entire dump truck full of the white, granular goodness.

Ludvig was pulling four pieces of crispy Ezekiel bread from the toaster to place on his plate. Next to the bread were six scrambled eggs and an eight-ounce steak, medium rare. He plopped his impressive bulk on the stool next to Magni at the kitchen bar.

"A pattern? Dat seems odd," Ludvig said as he shoveled a fourth of his eggs into his salivating mouth.

"Why?"

Ludvig nodded his chin over to Magni's phone, which currently had the map app open showing red pins in an almost perfect line. As he cut a huge chunk of the juicy steak, he pondered aloud, "Why a straight line like dat?" Teeth scraped on the metal fork as the meat was heartily consumed, followed by a chug of organic whole milk.

"That's good for us, isn't it?"

"Mmph," Ludvig replied, neither answering nor ignoring the question. "Where would you set up de trap, apprentice?" The Hunter already had a place picked out in his mind, but wanted this to be a teachable moment.

"Here," answered the eager teenager, pointing to a local park seemingly in the middle of the path.

"Right," Ludvig said, prompting Magni to sit a little straighter with a smile adorning his face. "And wrong." The teenager shrunk back down as his grin faded.

"Wh—"

"Right, because it is away from de human's homes, but wrong due to it still being dangerously close."

"Oh, right," Magni agreed while nodding his head and squinting at the screen again. "The wolves could flee and run right into a home, especially if they are hurt and need meat to heal."

"Exactly," Ludvig said with a smile that was almost spilling the copious amounts of protein he was shoveling. A massive hand patted the much smaller teenager on the back a few times, prompting the boy to swell up with pride again. Ludvig let him have his moment.

"So we bait the park and then lure them into the industrial area over here," Magni said while moving the map and swirling his finger around an area of commercial warehouses. "No one should be there late at night."

"Very good," Ludvig said as he finished his plate. Magni sometimes wondered if his master ate purely for nourishment to the point where he didn't even get to enjoy his food. He recalled the Hunter informing his apprentice that you were most vulnerable in three scenarios: shitting, sleeping, and eating. Magni also thought taking a shower made one fairly vulnerable, but had decided that, given how many centuries Ludvig had been alive, he had been referring to times way back before the advent of showers.

Rinsing off his plate before placing it and the empty cup in the dishwasher, Ludvig turned and scowled at the still half-full bowl of cereal before the young man.

"You're never going to grow big and strong if you don't eat," Ludvig said while crossing his arms over his chest.

"I've never been a big breakfast eater, you know that."

"We will have to train your body to eat on a schedule. Now, finish your schoolwork before we get ready for de hunt."

"Where are you going?" Magni asked, bringing up another spoonful of the high-fiber cereal.

Ludvig had moved the rug in the living room and was preparing to go down through the iron door that was built into the floor. To Magni, it looked like a manhole cover.

Once unlocked, Ludvig opened the hatch and began going down the ladder as he said, "I need to prepare de rooms for our guests."

Magni got up from his stool and rushed to look down at his master before saying, "You mean we are going to capture them alive?"

Looking up from the darkness, Ludvig said, "Yes, Magni. Normally we would simply execute de offending supernatural and burn de remains, but dis feels different. I want to know who—or what—we are dealing wif." Magni smiled inwardly at his master's English and how he sometimes replaced *th* words with *f* or *d* almost interchangeably. At times, Lude would say "wid" instead of "with," while other times he would use "wif." Then again, the guy spoke, like, five languages while Magni spoke only one, so who was he to say anything.

Ludvig disappeared beneath the manhole cover and a light flipped on. Magni slowly crouched down to get a better look when Ludvig called out, "Schoolwork!"

"Ah, man," Magni let out in an exhale as he grabbed his stack of books and sat on the couch. With a scowl, he opened them and began doing the practice test from the day before.

Later that night, and with the van fully loaded with werewolf-specific restraints, they were off.

After around an hour and forty-five minutes of driving, they arrived at the park.

"Lay de bait at the edge, just past dose trees," Ludvig said while pointing through the windshield. "Den meet me at de warehouse park."

"Industrial park," Magni corrected. Ludvig just looked at him for a moment before gesturing with his head to get moving.

Grabbing the plastic-lined duffel bag filled with fresh meat slabs from the butcher, Magni began lugging his bait to the edge of the park. The van pulled away, leaving the teenager alone in the dark.

The hair instantly stood up on the back of his neck, prompting the boy to pick up his pace. The meat bag was heavy and he had to drastically lean away from it to maintain his balance.

Within a few minutes, Magni arrived at the edge of the park, where he zipped open the duffel and grabbed the largest piece of meat he could find. Dropping the slab, he began carefully walking into the wooded area that separated the park from the commercial area. Magni had never understood why Houston was so lax with its zoning laws. There could be a hopscotch of commercial zones, residential, and back again for miles.

There came the rustling of a bush from behind, which caused Magni's breath to catch while simultaneously clenching his butt cheeks. Slowly pivoting around, the image of Ludvig chastising him for acting too cautiously sprang to mind, and Magni expertly pulled the Glock free from its thigh holster before jerking his body around to face the noise.

A raccoon came lumbering out, following the scent of the meat, allowing for Magni's stuck breath to squeeze past his relaxing throat. Holstering his weapon with a nervous smile and a shake of his head, Magni turned back around and proceeded to make his way toward the edge of the park. He could see the warehouses through the trees up ahead.

A growl that sounded like rolling thunder in the distance danced fingertips made of ice up Magni's spine. Dropping the bag, the apprentice supernatural hunter began sprinting for the tree line and the safety of his master. His breath instantly turned into shallow gasps as terror filled his veins like a nitro-boosted racing car.

An ear-splitting howl that sounded eerily like a haunted ghost train rang out, followed by two more in answer. Ferocious barks filled the night like machine guns as more shrubbery rustled violently.

"LUDVIG!!!" Magni shrieked as he ran, waving his arms and unintentionally slowing his speed. The van was fifty or sixty feet ahead, parked at the edge of the parking lot where the lush grass ended.

The unmistakable sound of pursuing gallops thudded the ground from behind, turning Magni's shuddering breaths into high-pitched wheezes. As he got closer to the vehicle, he could see himself bounding in the reflection of the tinted windows. A few yards behind him, Magni's wide, terrified eyes could make out three lumbering shapes chasing after him.

"DROP!"

Magni did as instructed without question, relying solely on muscle memory as his mind was flooded with conflicting signals. Smacking the ground from a sprint, all the air was bashed from his torso, but that was the least of his worries at the moment.

A small explosion rang out and Magni felt something whoosh over his prone body.

There was a cry of surprise as something hit one of the wolves.

Ludvig dropped to the ground from where he had jumped on top of the van for a clear shot, letting go of his net launcher as he did. The weapon clattered to the ground as the Hunter pulled a chrome air gun filled with tranquilizer darts specifically made for supes.

Without a moment's hesitation, the Hunter began sending darts downrange with the *hiss* of compressed air while storming forward to step over his protégé. The darts hit home as a white wolf with a black patch over one eye yelped in surprise. The much larger dark brown wolf continued to charge forward, as if the darts had been merely filled with saline.

"*Skit!*" he cursed in Swedish as he dropped the chrome-plated pistol and pulled out his wand, juking to the side with incredible speed no ordinary human could reproduce. As the wolf leaped through the air to where it thought Ludvig was going to be, the Swede rolled in the opposite direction, bringing his glowing wand up to bear and springing back to his feet in an instant. The wand shot out an arc of electricity that smashed into the soaring wolf, throwing it off its initial trajectory to spin in the air while flying sideways.

"Get de tranq rifle!" Ludvig commanded as the white wolf crashed into him, snapping at his meaty forearm. The Swede let the wolf gnaw on his armor-covered appendage, knowing full well lycanthropes took what they could and usually preferred throats or arms. The wolf growled in fury as teeth the size of AAA batteries snapped at the iron-infused Kevlar coating his coat.

Ludvig brought his glowing wand up to point directly at the wolf, but a paw swiped out, knocking the wood from his grasp while also shredding through the leather glove and the flesh of his hand.

"ARGH!" Ludvig cried out between gritted teeth as he reached with bleeding fingers to wrap around the wolf's throat and squeeze. Twin yellow orbs with slits down the middle went wide in surprise as the Hunter began choking the life from the wolf with hands as strong as vises.

He started getting to his feet, lifting the wolf off the ground while it pawed at the air, claws raking on the Kevlar wrapped around the Swede's forearms.

With his free hand, he pulled out the Glock with the iron resin shots, aimed it at the wolf's forehead, and then pulled the weapon away. Pointing the muzzle at one of the back legs instead, Ludvig pulled the trigger just as a black wolf with a white patch on his eye slammed into the man from behind.

The white wolf dropped to the ground, yelping loudly from surprise and pain as it tried to stand up on all fours. The shot had only been a flesh wound, but a deep one that spewed blood.

Ludvig was on his stomach trying to turn on his back when the black wolf began digging into his body armor like a dog digging for a juicy bone in the yard.

A *hiss* of compressed air pierced the night and the black wolf stopped digging and yelped in surprise. This gave Ludvig all the time he needed to push off the ground in a forcible roll, throwing the werewolf off balance.

As the Hunter was cleared from danger, he pulled out his rune-covered cold-iron katana and swiped down at the black wolf near its rump. The blade bit into flesh and cut a line down the thigh muscle, which began oozing blood. Ludvig knew that as long as it wasn't spurting, he would probably live.

The brown wolf, which was noticeably larger than the other two, was on his feet and leaping toward the teenage boy.

"MAGNI!" Ludvig bellowed in fear-laced warning. The apprentice turned and shot his weapon from the hip as the big wolf crashed into him, knocking him easily to the ground. His head bounced off the concrete curb, rendering him unconscious.

From the corner of his vision, Ludvig was aware that the white wolf was slowly collapsing to the ground, lowering its head and taking shallow breaths, the initial darts finally taking hold.

The black wolf was whining as it tried to limp away, leaving only the enormous brown were, who Ludvig was confident was the largest he had ever seen. The thing was eight feet in length from the tip of its nose to the base of its tail and had to weigh at least two hundred and twenty kilos, judging by the Swede's past experiences with werewolves.

With blazing yellow eyes, the brown were—the alpha—leaned down and opened dripping jaws to wrap around Magni's exposed, tender throat.

"Wait! He's only a child!" Ludvig cried out with an outstretched hand, his other slowly patting for the Glock that wasn't in its holster. He knew it had been knocked to the ground when the black wolf had pounced.

To his surprise, the wolf paused and slowly began pulling its glistening teeth away from the unconscious boy while intelligent yellow orbs regarded the Swede. The pupil slits were opening and closing sporadically, and Ludvig knew the dart sticking out of the beast's chest was working. That and the several others that had landed in the initial attack.

"Who are you?" Ludvig asked as he stood up, still holding a hand out. His other went for the belt buckle that contained a silver knife. He held it in a closed fist that oozed blood, and it stuck out between the middle and ring fingers.

In answer, the wolf lunged through the air, but noticeably slower than before. Ludvig danced to the side while slashing at the wolf's legs, digging a shallow trench in its flesh. Once again, Ludvig was surprised as the wolf didn't even yelp in pain.

As the monster landed, Ludvig spotted his wand and dove, doing a roll as he picked up the wooden weapon. Springing to his feet, the Hunter turned right as the wolf was about to lunge again.

Ludvig sent a shower of electricity where he thought the wolf was going to be, only to figure out too late that he had been tricked. Instead of going for the throat as most wolves did, the were plunged into the Swede's legs, bending his knees backward with a sickening pop that was felt as much as heard.

The Swede roared in agony as the wolf mounted the man and brought fangs up to drip saliva on the Hunter's face.

"*Skit*," the Swede cursed again in an exhale as wide eyes locked with yellow orbs. The beast swallowed the thick man's neck easily and began clamping down just as the were's eyes began to flutter and his breathing went shallow.

The werewolf lost consciousness and collapsed on top of Ludvig, sending all his air out in a shotgun blast as the man was crushed under five hundred pounds of monster.

Or maybe it wasn't a monster? It had spared the boy.

With shuddering breaths from indescribably agony, Ludvig bench-pressed the wolf off of him and rolled him to the side with a grunt of both pain and effort. Lude had always used his feet to press off the ground when benching, and having his knees broken while his body tried to use muscle memory and push off *really* fucking hurt.

Once the wolf was on the ground and breathing heavily, Ludvig dropped his head to the soft grass and took deep, steadying lungfuls of air, concentrating on blocking out the pain signals that demanded to be heard.

A growl came from his side and the black wolf limped toward the downed man, who was helpless to stop him. He had dropped the wand and knife somewhere and knew the game was up.

A *hiss* rang out and a silver dart landed in the front leg of the black wolf, who barked in fury before making a renewed lunge toward the helpless Swede.

Yellow eyes began to flutter, as this wolf was considerably smaller than the alpha, and he dropped to the ground.

Ludvig lifted his head to regard his apprentice, who was dropping the muzzle of the rifle he held while in a seated position. His free hand went up to the back of his head, and he pulled away fingers coated in crimson.

Pushing himself to painfully rest on his bottom, Ludvig placed both hands over one knee and closed his eyes. A bright white light spilled between his fingers, illuminating the darkness as bones popped, prompting the man to cry out.

Once the job was done, he moved to the other knee, took in a deep breath, and repeated the process, nearly passing out as it popped back into place. Spittle squeezed between gritted teeth and ran down a cleanly shaven square chin.

After he was healed, Ludvig wanted to drop back onto the grass and rest his eyes for a bit, as healing his injuries had taken a lot of precious energy, but he knew he didn't have the luxury. Instead, he pushed himself up to his feet, testing out his repaired legs, and made his way to his apprentice.

With another quick focus, white light escaped from between clasped hands and Magni's head stopped bleeding, the skin knitting itself closed.

"Wow," Magni drawled out as he stared at his master. He had never seen him use that much healing magic before.

"Perks of being a paladin-mage, huh?" Ludvig said as he extended his hand out to his apprentice.

Magni took it and got to his feet, still staring in awe at his master. "I still don't understand how you can be both."

"We went over dis, apprentice. All people can use elemental magic if dey only know how to harness de power."

"I know, I know. People use it all the time to heal themselves of cancer and stuff just by meditating. I've seen the documentaries. What do they call it? Okra?"

"Chakra. Dey aren't wrong, but dere's more to it dan dey fink. Now, grab de small ones. Make sure to muzzle dem first," he commanded before opening the back and side doors of the van. Magni climbed into the back and reached for the three muzzles and six sets of restraints, all made of silver.

Stepping out, he threw one muzzle and two cuffs to his master, who caught them with alternating hands. Working with practiced efficiency, the Swede secured the large brown wolf before removing the darts and dragging him to the side door of the van. With a grunt, the large man hefted the five-hundred-pound wolf into the van and tethered its muzzle in place with a six-inch lead.

Magni tried to pull the smaller white wolf—who was probably only around a hundred and sixty kilos, Ludvig thought—but he wasn't strong enough.

"Dis is why you need to eat," Ludvig said as he approached the first wolf, who had already been muzzled and cuffed, grabbed him by the scruff, and easily dragged him over to the black wolf. With barely a gritting of his teeth, he hoisted the white wolf in, shoved him to the side, and lifted the black one after. Magni just watched in awe as Ludvig handled the three-hundred-and-fifty-pound wolves like they were merely large bags of lawn clippings or something.

"Dese must be de twins," Ludvig said as his eyes drifted from the white wolf with a black patch over one eye to the black wolf with the white patch.

Once the three wolves had been secured in place, Ludvig shut the doors while Magni retrieved any evidence and weaponry. After the pair slid into the van, the teenager handed his master the Glock, wand, sword, and silver belt knife that he had found on the ground.

"Fank you."

"Fank?" Magni asked, rolling the words over his tongue. "Oh, thank. Got ya."

"Dat's what I said. Thank," Ludvig answered, enunciating the th sound this time around. It sounded weird to Magni.

He pressed the ignition on the electric van and they were off.

CHAPTER 4

Depweg awoke in a room that was bathed in inky blackness. He rubbed at his eyes, feeling how heavy they were, and hoped that they were still waking up.

Opening them again, he was rewarded with absolute darkness. He waved a hand in front of his face and couldn't even see it with his preternatural eyes. If he shifted, he might be able to see something with his pupils as slits instead of dots, which made it easier to hunt at night.

Nostrils flared as Depweg began making his way around the room, feeling the cold concrete of the wall. He rapped his knuckles against the stone and sensed nothing on the other side. He deduced that either the walls were surprisingly thick or they were underground.

Something nagged at him, and his fingers explored his own body to discover a bandage on his shoulder. It was tender to the touch and seeped warm plasma. He immediately knew the knife had been silver or iron, as most other wounds healed with relative ease.

Feeling the wall, Depweg's fingers touched cold metal, and he knew immediately that it was a door made of magic-canceling iron. His claws would break against the material if he shifted.

Lowering his head to the ground, Depweg stuck his nose as close to the gap as possible, inhaling deeply. Dawson and Joey were nearby, and that gave him a spark of hope.

"Boys," Depweg loudly whispered. "Boys, can you hear me?"

There was a slap of flesh on concrete followed by a moan. Depweg could picture a cell across the hall with one of the twins coming to and feeling around like he had just done.

"Joey, Dawson. Can you hear me?"

"Ugh," Dawson answered from across the hall. Though they were twins, they had different mannerisms and ways of speaking that made it obvious who was who once you got to know them.

"What the hell, man?" Joey asked in a cell next to Depweg. "Where are we?" he asked through a pained groan.

"I don't know, but we aren't dead yet. So that's good," the alpha tried to reassure his pack.

There was the sound of metal swinging on a hinge, followed by steps down a ladder somewhere to Depweg's right. A light was switched on, and Depweg had to slam his eyes shut while covering his face with his hands to block the bright beams that slipped through the crack under the door.

In only a few moments his eyes readjusted, and Depweg lowered his face to the ground again, peering out as best he could.

There was the sound of a door opening, followed by heavy footfalls on the concrete floor. Depweg could see military-style boots approaching his cell and he pushed himself to a standing position.

A narrow window opened in the door and the square face of a blond man with blue eyes peered in with a scowl.

"Who are you? What do you want with us?" Depweg demanded while shifting on his feet, feeling his body preparing for fight or flight.

Blue eyes continued to stare appraisingly. It unnerved Depweg that this man, this mortal, had bested him and the twins so easily.

"What is your name?" the man demanded, ignoring Depweg's question.

Having nothing to hide, the were alpha responded with, "Jonathan Depweg. We work with Father Thomes Philseep." The names meant very little to Ludvig, though he was sure he had heard of Depweg before, even before the man in white had mentioned him. "We are good guys," he finished, holding his hands out to his captor, palms up in a show of placation. "I-I think you're a good guy, too. Otherwise we'd be dead. Plus, you love that boy. It's been my experience that bad guys in the field don't usually care about one another."

Their captor continued to stare with a stoic gaze that pierced Depweg's very soul.

"Why did you hurt all dose people?"

"We didn't. We were following the trail because we were wondering the same thing."

The blue eyes continued to peer at Depweg before the window slammed shut and harsh footsteps disappeared down the hallway he guessed they were in. A door shut and the lights went off before the sound of someone going up a ladder rang out in the darkness. A protest of metal on hinges, and their prison was secured.

Depweg walked over to the far wall, placed his back against it, and slid down to his butt. He knew they were in for the long haul.

Sometime later, Depweg didn't know how long, the hatch opened again, followed by muffled talking and the descent of someone down the ladder. The light was switched on and Depweg shielded his eyes before he could be blinded, choosing to let a little bit slip through his fingers until his pupils adjusted.

The door at the end of the hall opened and the big man walked down its length to stop at Depweg's door. He slid open the window and pushed in a Styrofoam tray.

Depweg hesitantly got to his feet and walked over to where the man was watching from the small gap. The were thought he could trust the man, as he wasn't dead yet and his captor had had every opportunity to kill them while Depweg and his pack had been under.

Taking the tray, Depweg walked back to the far wall and sat cross-legged as he examined the food by the light shining through the window that the man had left open intentionally. Another indication that the man was on the good side—at least Depweg hoped.

There were no utensils on the tray, but a nice, juicy New York strip looked back up at Depweg, beckoning him.

After several sniffs with his sensitive nose, Depweg picked up the steak and began taking tentative bites. It was delicious, and even had a garlic butter marinade on top, not that the weres needed the topping; it was still a nice touch.

The captor had moved on to the other cells and was offering Dawson food when Depweg heard his packmate call out, "No fucking way, man. Shove it up your ass, or whatever."

"Dawson," Depweg called out loudly, "it's fine. Take the food."

"You're lucky I need to heal, bitch," Dawson said defiantly as Depweg heard the tray scrape against the window.

The man turned and repeated the process, giving Joey a tray, who took it without a word. Joey had always been the quieter, less emotional of the twins.

The light of Depweg's cell was momentarily swallowed by darkness as the large man walked by his window.

"Wait!" Depweg called out, swallowing the rest of the steak. To his surprise, the man moved back toward the door, blotting out the light again with his bulk.

"Who are you? At least tell me your name."

"Ludvig, de Hunter," the large man answered before abruptly resuming his path out of the prison. Because that's where they were. A prison.

Ludvig closed the door but didn't turn off the light this time. Footsteps sounded as he ascended the ladder before closing the hatch to the outside world, and their freedom.

"Ludvig," Depweg mouthed, tasting the name and cementing it in his brain.

"What does he want with us?" Depweg heard Joey ask softly, as if he had spoken the words aloud only for himself.

"I don't know, but don't do anything stupid and we might make it out of here."

"Ya, Joey. Don't do anything stupid, alright, bruh?" Dawson chided. Depweg knew his rebelliousness was a direct reflection to their helpless circumstances; much like how John tried to inject humor into awkward situations.

"John," Depweg breathed out as his head hung low and he placed his elbows on his knees where he sat. He had been gone nine years and wouldn't be coming to save the day this time. Nine. Fucking. Years.

"You miss him, don't ya?" Dawson asked softly, which was uncharacteristic of the young were.

"Didn't mean for you to hear that, boys," Depweg answered while rubbing a hand down his face.

"It's cool," Joey said. "We didn't know him for very long, but he was still pretty alright, even for a bloodsucker."

Depweg placed a hand over his mouth and lost the battle over his emotions. For the first time, Depweg quietly sobbed, missing his best friend of nearly a hundred years. He had kept himself busy over the last nine years by working with Father Thomes and picking up where John had left off in his abrupt absence. He hadn't taken a day off, opting to either work or be around his pack as much as he could, never realizing it was all a distraction. But now, here, in the solitude of his cell, Depweg wept. Though he was as quiet as possible, Joey and Dawson knew what their alpha was going through and decided not to say anything.

Tears ran down his flushed cheeks as he cupped his mouth in an attempt to silence his crying. The smell of cooked steak flooded his nose, temporarily pulling him from his sullen stupor.

"I'm sorry, boys," Depweg called out, refusing to let the situation be awkward by calling out exactly what was happening. Depweg fully believed that things only became weird if you let them.

"For what?" Joey asked.

"For losing my shit for a minute. An-and for getting you guys caught. It's my fault."

"How's that? Pretty sure we wanted to go with you," Dawson answered. Depweg could hear the confused scowl on his face.

"I never stopped to think about . . . about losing my best friend. He's gone, and I need to accept that. I-I've been so busy trying to fill my life with work that I never stopped to just grieve. Had I done so, I . . . I don't think we would be here. I would have taken more time to plan and noticed something was wrong. Instead, I just sprinted toward danger, feeling like it was somehow my fault that he's gone."

"No offense, but cut that shit out, alright?" Dawson said with a tone that was both harsh and respectful.

"Yeah, we followed you because we wanted to, man," Joey added.

"Besides, we've done a lot of good in the past nine years working with Papa T," Dawson reminded his alpha. A pang of sorrow flitted across Depweg's chest like a plucked guitar string at the mention of Papa T. That had always been John's name for Father Thomes, knowing it was annoying to the old timer even if the priest didn't say so.

"Thank you, boys," Depweg said as he wiped his face, flinching as he moved his shoulder.

"What do you think he wants with us?" Joey asked, changing the subject.

"I don't know. Just . . . just do as he says and we will be alright. And Dawson?"

"Yeah?"

"Be respectful."

"Aw, man," Dawson drawled in genuine dismay.

"This guy has the keys to our freedom. I don't know why, but I think he doesn't want to kill us."

"Could have fooled me," Dawson responded. Depweg thought he could hear the were's eyes roll.

Sleep eventually came and pulled the three under the waves of consciousness.

The sound of metal clanging woke Depweg up with a start, and he rubbed his eyes in confusion at where he was. It only took a few moments to remember the situation he was in, right as the window to his cell slid open.

A pair of silver cuffs was thrown in, followed by a terse command, "Put dese on and stand facing de wall. If you move, I will shoot you. Do you understand?"

"I understand," Depweg answered as he put on the cuffs in front of his body and turned to stand in the corner. Depweg didn't bother putting them on behind his back because he understood the point was to not let the were change out of his man-suit rather than a restriction of movement.

The door opened and the large man walked to the opposite corner of where Depweg stood, and set down a sloshing bucket.

He returned to the door, closing it, before saying, "Bring your hands here."

Depweg turned and walked to the door, sticking his hands up and through the tight-fitting window. There were some clicks, and the cuffs came off.

"Don't suppose you would be willing to give us some clothes," Depweg asked, glancing down at his naked frame.

"I'll consider it," was his answer.

Depweg turned and looked at the bucket in the corner.

"It's clean water. Use it to drink, bathe, and wash your waste down de drain in de center. And here," Ludvig said as something was stuck through the window. "Here's some soap, a plastic razor, and a toofbrush."

"Are we supposed to use the soap to brush our teeth, ass?" Dawson yelled.

"Dawson," Depweg called out, hushing the were. The captor squinted in response to the alpha before closing the window.

Ludvig repeated the process, with Depweg looking out from the small crack at the bottom of the door, silently willing Dawson to stay quiet and not try anything foolish against this powerful opponent.

At night, Ludvig brought more food before asking Depweg a few more questions, and then leaving again without offering anything in return.

It went on like that for some time. Depweg didn't know exactly how long, but he guessed it was several weeks to a few months at least. At some point, the large man had given each of the prisoners a loose set of clothes.

During their conversations, Ludvig had asked about Father Thomes, their predilection for only killing bad guys, and their allies. Depweg had intentionally kept his friends out of the conversation, except for Father Thomes, whose reputation he was banking on. Plus, he didn't think it pertinent to mention their warlock friend, as they were considered to be on the wrong side, usually.

One night, or maybe it was day, Depweg flat out asked, "Why are we here? What are you going to do with us?" There was a finality to his voice that hinted that there would be consequences of one form or another if Ludvig didn't at least give him that.

"I need to keep you here so de outside world finks you dead. I was told if I killed you, den we would be given de location of de vampyr."

"Jo-John?" Depweg stammered, his head getting light with the revelation that his best friend was potentially still alive.

Ludvig's eyes squinted harshly as he regarded his captive.

"How do you know him?"

"He's my best friend."

Ludvig's eyebrows went up in surprise before returning to their scowling position.

"Wha-what do you want with him?"

"To kill him for what he has done," Ludvig answered, testing Depweg.

"Look," Depweg started while lifting both his hands in placation, doing his best to show no hostility, "if you kill him, you'll start the apocalypse. Okay?"

Ludvig marinated on what the were had said before spitting out, "Explain, now." The Swede had known about the prophecy overall, and now wanted the one closest to the vampire to reveal more details of the puzzle.

"'When the last vampire walks the Earth, the gates of Hell will open.' Yo-you can't kill him without killing everyone on the planet. Not to mention all the souls that have ever existed since the dawn of time."

Ludvig continued to stare with dubious eyes that concealed a hidden wrath should he be lied to. Ludvig's worst fear was being confirmed by someone in the know.

"You have to believe me, Ludvig," Depweg said, using his captor's name to try and build a rapport. "Let me ask you something: whoever told you about us, do you think they were after my pack, or John?"

Ludvig thought about his encounter with the thing that had said it was an angel, letting his eyes go unfocused. Depweg caught this and continued.

"A lot of people want John dead, believe me," Depweg almost chuckled as he spoke. "But they want the end of everything. You are being used to start Armageddon, my friend. You are clearly good at what you do," he said while humbly gesturing down at himself. "Why else would they need you? Many, *many* have tried to assassinate my best friend. But he is notoriously difficult to kill. Hell, it's more likely he will destroy *himself* rather than someone else doing it."

"Why should I believe anyfing you say?" Ludvig demanded coldly, but with a lack of true conviction. "Which is more likely? De fact dat you are protecting your friend, or dat his deaf will cause Ragnarök?"

Depweg, sensing Ludvig's hesitation, offered, "I get what you are saying, Ludvig, I really do. And instead of trying to convince you otherwise, I will simply suggest you go talk to him."

Ludvig's head rocked back slightly at the suggestion, as if Depweg had pushed on his forehead ever so gently.

After a few heartbeats of looking in, Ludvig felt the need to confess something to this likable werewolf.

"I'm only going to say dis once," he sighed as he rubbed his forehead. "I didn't fink I had a choice in keeping you here. It was either dis or I killed you. For what it's worf, I'm glad I didn't."

"I understand," the captive replied with complete sincerity.

Without another word, Ludvig shut the window and made his way out of the prison and up the ladder.

Depweg smiled to himself knowing that if John was still alive, he'd be able to win Ludvig over. John had that quality about him that Depweg couldn't quite put his finger on.

Stepping back to the wall, Depweg slid down until he was sitting again, hope blossoming in his chest.

Chapter 5

Ludvig closed the hatch to the prison while Magni was studying on the couch. He was hanging upside down with his legs hung over the top cushion and his head almost resting on the floor.

Magni looked over to see his friend's screwed-up face and righted himself, almost passing out from lifting himself upright so quickly.

"What?" the apprentice asked, sensing something was off.

"Nofing. I need to go for a drive. Finish your studies and den you can watch TV."

"Can I play Nintendo?"

"Hmm? Sure, I don't care," Ludvig responded while shutting the front door behind him.

Magni heard the car door shut as the van started up and drove down the dirt road.

"Hmph," Magni breathed while he closed his book and picked up his handheld Nintendo. He turned on the TV and began playing a game that had a kid with a green hat and a floating fairy that gave him advice. It always reminded him of Raziel, and he missed his friend dearly.

Ludvig drove in silence with only the sound of the road as his companion. Not even the radio dared make a peep. What worried the man the most was the confirmation that the rumors of Ragnarök were true. He couldn't find a comfortable position as he drove, shifting in his seat constantly.

After an indeterminate amount of driving, because the man had been lost in a churning ocean of thought, Ludvig arrived at where he had killed the rogue troll. He got out of the van and marched confidently into the forest, armed only with his wand and the silver knife on his belt buckle that he knew wouldn't offer any help.

Once in the woods, Ludvig bellowed, "ANGEL! I HAVE KILLED DE WOLVES. COME TO ME."

"Now, now, now, no need to yell," said the beautiful man with glowing eyes and hair the color of wheat dancing in the sun. His white suit was pristine and expensive looking. "Where are the wolves?" the angel asked while making a show of looking around.

"Dey are dead. Now where is de vampyr?" Ludvig lied, crossing his huge arms over his chest.

The angel looked dubiously at him, assessing him with eyes that held immense intelligence built over the eons.

"I don't believe you," the angel said coldly, tilting his head down so that he was peering at Ludvig almost through his glowing eyebrows.

"I removed dem from de board nearly a year ago." Ludvig knew the only way to sell a lie was to include some truth.

"They had better stay removed, Ludvig Mansson, or I will do to you what I did to your entire pantheon." The Swedish man's mouth dropped at the realization he was referring to the Norse gods, who had been murdered violently.

As the beautiful man finished, four ivory horns pierced through the flesh of his skull at even points around his skull. Two grew from his temples while the remaining set sprouted from somewhere behind his skull. They grew a full foot into the air, with points breaking off at ninety degrees at the halfway mark to curl around in a circle. The points touched, forming an unholy halo in direct contrast to the angels above as unseen heat bloomed from the crown, making the top half dance in a haze.

Beautiful eyes became orbs of roiling hellfire, spilling green, red, and orange flames out of skull-like sockets. The white suit ripped, and bulging muscles expanded, covered in a road map of pulsating red veins. Skin the color of blackened leather glowed like the embers of freshly lit charcoal, and goat legs lifted the being higher into the sky. Obsidian hooves that glowed like a blacksmith's creation fresh from the forge burned the foliage where he stood. Leather wings akin to a dragon's expanded outward for twenty feet.

Ludvig stared with wide, terrified eyes as Lucifer, Lord of Hell, spoke with a voice that sounded like mountains grinding together.

"Kill the vampire and I will spare your pathetic existence, puny being. Betray my commands, and I will erase you from existence. Eternal nothingness will be your tomb, with maddening silence as your only companion. Besides," Satan smiled with fierce eyes, "we both know what happens when you die, don't we?"

Ludvig's mouth went dry as his throat constricted and anxiety tightened his chest, suffocating him. This . . . this monster had killed the Norse gods. How could Ludvig dare to stand a chance against the might of the most powerful angel that had ever existed when even Odin—the strongest of the Norse—had fallen?

With a single tear slipping past his orders to not weep at the loss of his beloved pantheon, Ludvig nodded his head once, lowering his face in shame. "I understand, Satan," he shuddered while uttering the name.

The man in white was there again when Ludvig found the strength to face his worst fear.

"Please, call me Samael," the beautiful man said as he stuck his hand out while wearing a shark's grin. Ludvig hesitantly gripped it, setting in play events that could never be undone.

The End

Jane versus the Black Knight

C.T. Phipps

This story is set in the Bright Falls Mysteries series.

Chapter 1

"Let me get this straight," I said, staring at the man across the table from me at the Deerlightful Diner. "You want to find Charlemagne's sword—"

"Joyeuse," Doctor Chuck Pepinson said. He was a pale, balding man with a goatee, dressed in a Grateful Dead T-shirt, jean shorts, and sandals. He was also a vampire. "The one in the Louvre is a fake. It's younger than Charlemagne by about two centuries."

"And you came to Bright Falls, Michigan to find it?" I asked, confused.

The Deerlightful Diner was an old-style 1950s diner with checkerboard print tiles and a circular bar. The diner had been cleared out for this meeting, as Doctor Chuck Pepinson had rented the place for an hour. It turned out it was because he wanted to have a meeting with me. I wasn't sure why until he told me the most ridiculous story I'd heard in years.

And I was a weredeer.

"Ms. Doe, I know it sounds strange—" Doctor Pepinson started.

"No, it sounds stupid," I interrupted, pausing. "Err, call me Jane. I don't mean any offense by this—"

"Some taken," Doctor Pepinson said, raising his hands. "However, I have reason to believe the sword fell into the hands of the Knights Templar after being looted from a Burgundy monastery by King Philip II to fight the Moors."

"Muslims," Jane said.

"Sorry," Doctor Pepinson apologized, pausing. "I was transformed at Berkley in the sixties, and we were just beginning the whole political correctness—"

"Please stop," I said, already bored with this conversation. I was already regretting agreeing to meet with the man. Well, not really, because I was deep in debt and just barely keeping the place open.

Doctor Pepinson took an entirely unnecessary breath. "The short version is, after the Knights Templar were driven underground, a small group of werewolf knights—"

"Werewolf knights?" I asked. Now the story was getting interesting.

"Yes, ancestors of the O'Henry clan," Doctor Pepinson said, speaking of a local family of werewolves. "They fled to Ireland and stayed there until the late 19th century. Then they immigrated to Bright Falls, Michigan, where they formed a marriage pact with the Finnigan werewolves."

"And they had Joyeuse with them?" I asked, wondering how he'd come up with such a crazy story.

Mind you, my revolver had been made from the melted down remains of Caliburn and was possessed by an angel, so maybe I wasn't one to talk. The Merlin Gun, as it was called, occasionally talked to me and gave me advice on what to kill.

This time, it was silent.

"Yes," Doctor Pepinson said, pulling out several books that looked like the kind Indiana Jones used. "But the family had internal conflicts. After the death of the old patriarch at the hands of Marcus O'Henry, his two other sons took the sword to be buried in the woods, as to deny the kinslayer his prize."

I blinked then pulled out my cell phone. "Stop right there. I'm going to verify your story right now."

"Uh, I'm not sure—"

"Shh!" I said, raising my pointer finger to shush him. I then called my best friend, Emma O'Henry, who was the spoiled but sweet daughter of the werewolf family that ruled Bright Falls, Michigan.

Emma picked up seconds later. "Hello?"

"Yeah, did your family used to have Joyeuse? The sword, not happiness," I asked, still certain I was being punked by the vampire across from me. I was half expecting Ashton Kutcher to pop out from behind a pair of bushes at any second—that would have made the whole thing worth it.

"Yes, we did!" Emma said cheerfully. "It was the sword used to anoint the Kings of the Werewolves until my grandfather lost it."

I blinked repeatedly. "I see."

"Yeah, the family would do almost anything to get it back," Emma said, her voice cheerfully ignorant of what was going on. "But it belongs in a museum."

I pulled my phone away, stared at it, and then put it back to my ear. "Yeah, thanks for that. Buh-bye."

"Wait, what—" Emma started to say.

I hung up.

"Are you satisfied?" Doctor Pepinson inquired, looking at me with a bored expression on his face. I caught a brief glimpse of his canines elongating in amusement.

"How the hell did you know all this?" I asked.

"One of Marcus' brothers recorded the story in a set of journals I acquired when he passed on. He was my co-chair of supernatural studies at the University of Los Angeles. I believe recovering the sword could be my crowning achievement as an archaeologist," Doctor Pepinson said, smugly.

"Recovering a sword that was apparently never really lost and you found exact directions to?" I asked, blinking. "Not exactly Indiana Jones material."

Doctor Pepinson frowned. "Would you accept that it'll still make me rich and famous?"

I blinked. "Yes, actually, I would."

"Well, I want to hire you to stand guard over my team as we excavate the hidden gravesite of William O'Henry to recover the sword," Doctor Pepinson said.

"Why me?" I asked, confused. "Also, shouldn't you be getting the permission of the family?"

"You have a certain reputation as a problem solver, even outside of Michigan," Doctor Pepinson said, coughing. "You allegedly have killed gods and ancient vampires."

I paused. "Would I get paid more or less if I said that was true?"

Doctor Pepinson gave a bemused smile. "As for the other part, the existing O'Henrys are descendants of the kinslayer branch of the family. They would also call what we're doing grave robbing."

"Probably because it is."

Doctor Pepinson shrugged. "Like all vampires, I have a certain level of moral flexibility."

"Because you're a damned evil spirit trapped in a corpse?"

"That's just racist," Doctor Pepinson said, narrowing his eyes before his expression returned to normal. "Also, very true. In any case, I am less worried about the O'Henrys than another problem that I hope you'll be able to help me deal with."

"Breakfast, lunch, and dinner?" I asked, looking around my diner. "Because, really, we could use the business."

"No," Doctor Pepinson replied, blanching. "It's something else."

***

"He wants you to be his dig's bodyguard?" Emma asked as she walked along the path toward the dig site in the middle of the woods. I had decided not to keep the robbing of her family's graves a secret from her, but instead had told her everything.

I'd just told her after Doctor Pepinson had set everything up and had been digging for two days. Okay, dick move, I know, but I had a good excuse for it: money. I felt guilty about it, but Emma was taking it surprisingly well.

My friend looked like one of the women you'd cast in a movie to play someone who existed in the real world. She was beautiful, with scarlet red hair, a generous figure, and perfect white skin. It was a side effect of being a shifter that the homeliest of us tended to be pretty while the beautiful were stunningly gorgeous. Unfortunately, I was more the former than the latter, and always felt a little self-conscious next to my network teen drama–looking friend. Today, she was wearing a pair of blue jeans and a House Stark T-shirt, but looked like she was modeling them. I was wearing the same, but looking considerably shabbier.

"Yes," I said, sighing. "He thinks your magic sword may be haunted and wants me to take care of it."

"Is it a magic sword?" Emma asked, looking over at me.

"I dunno. Don't you know?" I asked, assuming the sword would be magical because why not?

Emma shrugged. "I always assumed its value was purely symbolic. A way of proving that the werewolves of our family were of a superior stock, related to ancient kings."

"That you were purebred?" I asked.

Emma glared at me.

"What?" I said, putting a hand over my chest. "You wouldn't have respected me if I hadn't made that joke. You gave me too much of an opening."

"I'm pretty sure I would have, actually," Emma replied simply. "In any case, why does Doctor Pepinson think the site is haunted?"

"Something, something, blood curse by your great uncles, something, something, dark magic."

Emma stopped in midstep. "You didn't think to tell me about this earlier?"

I shrugged. "I'm telling you about it now."

Emma felt her face in embarrassment. "Blood curses are a big thing among werewolves."

"Well, I'm a weredeer, so I don't know about those sorts of things."

Emma took a deep breath. "You said he only knew about one of those brothers surviving?"

"Yes."

"It means the other was probably sacrificed to bring a terrible doom upon those who would disturb the grave."

I blinked, processing that information. "Huh, well, that would have been good to know a couple of days ago."

Emma stretched out her hands and made strangling gestures. "We need to keep him from digging it up."

"Right," I said, giving her a pair of thumbs-up. "Don't worry about it. We've got plenty of time to stop all of this. I'll do it, even if I have to give back half the money."

"Jane—"

"I know, I know!" I said, sighing. "It's just, you can exchange it for goods and services!"

Emma shook her head ruefully, right before there was a voice nearby that shouted, "We found it!"

"Oh, dammit," I muttered, rushing through the trees with Emma following close behind.

The two of us found ourselves in the middle of a grove that was full of a dozen university grad students around several dug-out plots that were cordoned off by stakes with string around them. In the middle one, Doctor Pepinson held up an ugly dirt-encrusted sword above an eaten-away skeleton buried in the ground.

This surprised me, not only for the fact that he'd managed to find the sword so quickly but because it was daytime, and the vampire should have been on fire. He hadn't been at the daylight portion of the dig until now, so I'd been happy to bring Emma here so we could deal with it while he was gone. The only vampires that could move around during the daytime were exceptionally old and powerful ones. That was when my brain caught up with my thoughts.

Oh, dammit. I'd been hustled.

"The power of the Second Empire is mine!" Doctor Pepinson shouted, sounding not at all dissimilar to a supervillain.

Above our heads, the sky clouded over and there was a crack of thunder. I felt a terrible wind pick up and wash over us. The supernatural energy in the air tripled and tripled again before becoming a blazing inferno of power. The various grad students, sensibly, all dropped their trowels and other tools to run in every direction but the one closer to their professor.

"That doesn't belong to you!" Emma shouted, perhaps missing the forest from the trees.

"Joyeuse is mine," Pepinson shouted, pointing the weapon at me. "It belongs to me by birthright!"

"It belongs to Charlemagne!" I shouted, doing my best impression of Indiana Jones.

"Exactly!" Pepinson cackled.

I blinked. "Seriously?"

Emma leaned over. "People were shorter back then. He also has the beard."

That was when the fog on the ground rolled over us, and a shadow emerged from it. The shadow shifted into the form of a black horse with blazing eyes. I instinctively labeled it a Nightmare because weredeer couldn't resist punning the way vampires couldn't resist counting and boggans couldn't resist betting.

On top of the horse, appearing with a flash of lightning, was a black-armored knight who looked straight out of the High Middle Ages. His plate mail was a lot more elaborate and beautiful than anything the Franks would have possessed in Charlemagne's time. Historical accuracy wasn't a huge concern with magic, after all.

"Destroy that ghost, Jane Doe!" Doctor Pepinson, Charlemagne, said. "It's what you are being paid for."

The Black Knight spoke, "Time has brought us together again, my king. Hell has no hold on my soul thanks to the curse woven on your blade. You will not wield it again, though. Its power belongs to one who has not betrayed his oaths!"

"Um, who the hell are you?" I asked, not sure if I should get involved in this.

"I am Roland," the Black Knight spoke. "Prefect of the Breton March, and he who was slain at the Battle of Roncevaux Pass."

"Ron-ce-what now?" I asked, stunned.

Emma, a lot more familiar with classical literature and history than me, spoke up, "Roland, hero of the Song of Roland? Why are you here? You should be in heaven! You're the original chivalric knight! The flower of chivalry! Everyone was inspired by your battle against the Basques!"

"A battle he lost!" Charlemagne hissed, displaying fangs. "The followers of Muhammad made a mockery out of my forces."

Roland conjured a lance out of thin air. "Poets have a way of making heroes out of villains and villains out of heroes. I began an invasion of the Basques land even though a peace treaty had already been negotiated between my emperor and Sulayman al-Arabi. I chose, instead, to slaughter and burn the villages of the heathen to create a war. I sought victory and glory by slaughtering God's enemies."

"Does he know Muslims worship the same God?" I asked Emma.

"I don't think he'd care," Emma responded. "They weren't fond of Jews in Roland's time either."

"You ruined my chance to rule Zaragoza and all of Spain!" Charlemagne hissed.

"I learned such vile tactics from you!" Roland hissed back. "You, who slaughtered all who dwelled in Verdun and yet were worshiped as greater than—"

"Bored now," I muttered, pulling out the Merlin Gun and shooting Roland off his horse with a single shot.

"Jane!" Emma shouted, shocked at my sudden attack.

"He's a damn ghost, blood curse thingy!" I shouted. "This conversation was never going to end well!"

"Ha!" Charlemagne laughed, still swinging his sword around.

I shot him in the face, sending the vampire tumbling backward. That was probably the only way I could have pulled it off, since Ancient Ones—vampires over a thousand years old—were effectively demigods in their strength and speed.

THAT'S NOT GOING TO STOP THEM, a booming voice spoke in my head. It was the Merlin Gun.

"Aren't you supposed to destroy these kinds of beings?" I asked.

THEY ARE BOTH POWERFUL, CURSED MEN. ALSO, NOW, VERY ANGRY.

Charlemagne was the first to stand up, his head glowing from the holy bullet inside his skull that was burning him from the inside out. "Betrayer! Harlot!"

"You okay?" I mocked. "You look like you have a little Ghost Rider thing going on there."

Charlemagne used vampire speed to cross the dig and grabbed me by the throat, lifting me up. "You will be the first to die by my blessed blade!"

That was when Emma turned into an enormous six-foot-tall wolf straight from Tolkien's nightmares and grabbed the ancient vampire by the throat, tearing him away from me. I fired a couple more shots in his back, unfortunately leaving me only two bullets even as he and Emma battled.

That was when I saw the Nightmare charging at me, its hooves causing puffs of hellfire to rise from the ground. I managed to get out of the way, but just barely.

Spinning around, I fired two more shots, missing one and hitting the demon horse with the last. It promptly exploded into a ball of fire and left me with one less foe to deal with.

"Wretched child of Lilith, you are an honorless piece of trash who shows no respect for your betters," Roland's voice spoke up from behind me.

"Have you ever heard it's not a good thing for villains to monologue?" I asked, spinning around and pulling the trigger on the Merlin Gun. Unfortunately, it didn't fire. No bullets left. Damn revolvers! I tossed it on the ground, which was probably not the best way to treat an angelically powered weapon, but you did what you had to do during life-and-death struggles.

Roland had his sword drawn and was slowly advancing on me. His helmet had fallen off to reveal a bearded man with a scarred visage that was far from the depiction of handsome French knights you saw in art about the period. In his hand was a hellish black iron copy of Durandal, the sister-sword to Joyeuse and Cortana (the last being a legendary sword as well as a Microsoft product). "I realize now, God will forgive me once I have turned my wrath against the supernatural. I am to guard Joyeuse against being taken, but I am at liberty to interpret my orders. I will slay thee, animate your corpse, and use it to wage war upon the heathen in this age."

I blinked. "You know, Rolo, I'm going to go out on a limb here and say you just don't get Christianity."

"Die!" Roland screamed, charging at me.

That was when I crouched down and made use of my epic deer-kicking power to kick the hell-spawned ghost in the chest, sending him backward on the ground. "Mixed martial arts, motherbucker!"

Roland sat up and opened his mouth before spewing out a fireball that I ducked under but still seared my hair and back. Thank God and the Goddess for weredeer reflexes, that was all I had to say.

"No fair, cheating!" I said, mocking the pretenses of the ghost.

"You will die!" Roland shouted, climbing up to his feet.

"You're a one-trick pony, you know that," I said, spotting Joyeuse on the ground. Emma and Charlemagne were still brawling, though I was putting my money on Emma, since his skin was starting to melt off while she was regenerating his attacks.

I pulled the magic sword to me with telekinesis, one of the few spells I knew and mostly useful for party tricks.

"No!" Roland hissed. "You are unworthy of that weapon."

"It's not the weapon; it's the woman."

He charged at me, so I hurled it at him and directed it with telekinesis to slam into his throat. I couldn't throw things very fast with my magic, but I could damn well make sure they went where I aimed. The sword slid through his neck and out through the other side, causing his spiritual form to dematerialize.

With that, I felt the oppressive aura around the dig site disappear. The clouds broke up as quickly as they'd arrived, and the wind died down. There was also no sense of magic left around the site. I looked down at Joyeuse and noticed the sword looked plain and unadorned. Not the sword of an emperor at all.

ROLAND WAS KIN TO CHARLEMAGNE. ITS POWERS WERE BROKEN WHEN USED AGAINST HIM, the Merlin Gun spoke.

"Whoops," I said.

Seconds later, I saw the head of Charlemagne rolling across the ground before crumbling to dust, as age tended to catch up with dead vampires. It was also possible the sunlight was affecting him now that he was dead.

Emma limped over to me in wolf form, having taken a bad beating even with her power to heal most wounds. "I got him."

"Good," I said, scratching behind her ears.

"What do we do with the sword?" Emma asked, swishing her tail around.

"You want it?"

"Hell no."

I nodded. "We'll think of something."

We ended up hanging it over the Deerlightful's jukebox.

The Sinking Man Series
Sheltered, Chapter 1

Justin S. Leslie

This is the first chapter out of my new Sinking Man series, a short series about zombies, based in Northeast Florida. It's not the typical fare in this space. Yes, the zombies are the problem, not everyone you run into. It's written to have several short novellas released throughout the year, and is focused and geared toward TV adaptation.

Side note, I used to do ghostwriting in this space. I know the genre . . .

Chapter 1

B EN STOOD LOOKING out over the St. Johns River from his secluded dock. Like most mornings, he held his cup of coffee in one hand and half-cocked attitude on life in the other. The out-of-the-way gated community he lived in, tucked away in a small inlet, secluded him from the apocalypse that was raging around him. At least, raging last time he had checked, which had been never.

Ben's morning walk didn't require him to wear pants—or underwear, for that matter—anymore. He leaned over with the robe he wore lightly pushed out of the way and released a splashing torrent, peeing directly into the water. The 9mm Glock hanging off a shoulder holster was the one thing he never forgot to wear. Pants yes, gun no.

Reaching down, Ben turned on the one thing he had that connected him to the world outside of his secluded, empty riverfront neighborhood: a satellite phone. He sighed, taking a sip of his coffee before shaking his head.

"Hello," was all he said into the receiver after dialing the last number he had called—the phone number his wife, Sarah, had given him before leaving. He'd learned that keeping the phone on all the time in hopes of receiving a call from her would only run the battery down over time, so with this knowledge, he only turned it on every morning while walking out to the dock, also sending a short text.

Two months ago to the day, he had received a text message saying nothing more than, "*The plan . . . safe.*" That message had reenergized Ben after almost ten months of complete seclusion. The plan was simple. Anything ever happened, they made their way home, no matter who was out or where they were.

The funny thing about apocalypses was that they had a peculiar sense of irony. Ben had struggled at first to figure out a name for what was happening, so he had hit the easy button and landed on zombies.

When it had first started, the world was calling them crazies. People catching a disease, then losing their shit. That had changed, though, and for the worse. People had started shifting and becoming, well . . . zombies of a sort.

Sarah, Ben's wife, worked for the CDC and had been called to work the case. Only this time, it hadn't been the regular routine of being gone for just a few weeks; this time, it had been months. She had gone to Denver and would go radio silent for weeks at a time. Meanwhile, the world had started to burn.

First, it had been in the news. So-called experts telling everyone to stay calm, only to have the news report rising numbers of infected at a staggering pace. In an effort to stop the spread, certain groups of people and areas had been slowly isolated, the full quarantine starting only a few weeks later. Only essential personnel had been allowed to function, slowly eroding the world's economies.

Soon, the general population had become restless, leading to riots and, what turned out even worse, people going back to their normal everyday lives out of necessity. The number of cases rose uncontrollably, overwhelming the health care system and collapsing it. This had only taken a few short months.

Then, the evacuations had started. As fast as the virus spread it started to mutate. Infected persons called crazies upon their imminent death changed to something even worse, something dead. Before the world stopped, it was reported that a trial vaccine caused the virus to change and mutate. When the vaccine did not resolve the issue, the evacuations began.

As a biomedical doctor, part of Sarah's job was to have a family care plan while she was away. Ben and Sarah had often binge-watched "Elite Preppers," a show for rich people that could afford to truly prep.

That faithful night six months before the shit hit the fan and she had been called away, the two of them had drunk multiple bottles of wine. Ben hated the stuff, but it always put the two in a mood for trouble. During a commercial break, an advertisement selling three years' worth of supplies and survival gear had appeared. It had also included a full solar kit and backup system for the house. All yours for the ripe old price of thirty thousand dollars. That night, they had bought the kit and mapped out their plans in case something ever did go down.

Ben let out a breath thinking about that night, taking the final sip of his coffee before sprinkling the rest on the ground. He turned, looking at the house as he did every morning. He fondly thought about the two of them calling the next day to cancel the order, only to find it nonrefundable, the effects of wine not in the cancelation policy.

Their house was nice by any standards a doctor would have. At five thousand square feet, it had plenty of room for what they had hoped would be a soon-to-grow family. As they were both in their midthirties, the clock had been ticking.

The solar panels gleamed off the back of the house, catching Ben's attention.

Since they couldn't get a refund on the drunken purchase, the two had decided to go all the way, adding a water filtration system to the list of upgrades. The house had been made for this.

"How ironic," Ben said to the air.

The neighborhood itself was relatively small, owning five other similarly large houses. It was a gated community, and designed to not draw attention to its semiwealthy owners, which included an ex-athlete, a local attorney, a retired couple whose house I had to visited yet, and a retired admiral. The turnoff was on a shaded two-lane road on the east side of the St. Johns River, south of the Buckman Bridge and Jacksonville, Florida.

If you didn't know the small neighborhood was there, you would miss the unimproved lane leading down to its entrance. The gate was ten feet tall, made of plaster block, and it wrapped around to the water's edge.

What made this property even better was that the houses sat back in a small cove, with docks at the back of each house only large enough to park a medium-sized ski boat. The trees, after not being maintained, had started to grow together at the opening of the cove. You could still see the houses, but if you weren't looking and passed by on a boat, you more than likely would miss the collection of nice households altogether.

When the evacuations had started, Ben had elected not to leave per their plan, staying put instead. This had ended up being the best possible scenario, since a couple weeks later, he'd heard jets overhead and what appeared to be bombs dropping in the area near Naval Air Station Jax, which had been the evacuation hub for the First Coast.

Sarah had always insisted on not leaving home in the case of a mass infection. *"Large masses of people are always a bad idea, and I wish people would stop doing it,"* rang in Ben's head as he walked up the final steps to the house.

In all fairness, it had taken several months for Ben to even feel the effects of the devastation around. Money could make even the end of the world a little more tolerable.

He was in a reflective mood. Maybe it was the fact that he was going to go through another house today. To date, he had only been through two others. The whole thing about, the devil next door had ended up taking on a true meaning after what he had found in one house, but that was for another day.

His neighbors had left on the first day of the evacuations, hoping to get a front-row seat to wherever it was they were going. Ben was betting on them never making it off the base. Television signals had been cut off later that week, leaving the rest up to Ben's imagination; only the noises he heard in the night being carried over the water, which could be from miles away, let him know anything about the outside world.

The watch on Ben's wrist came to life. "Good morning," the chirpy electronic voice of his smartwatch pronounced.

Ben pulled the watch to his mouth. "Morning. Set an alarm for noon. Label it 'house.'" The watch was the latest technology had to offer. It was programmable, and he had even sprung for the upgraded artificial intelligence application. Luckily for Ben, it didn't need the Internet. All he had to do was plug it into the computer and answer three hundred questions. The watch programmed itself from there. You could even adjust it to respond certain ways to phrases.

Set in his routine, Ben reprogrammed the conversation every month with simple phrases, that while scripted, made time pass.

"How are you?"

"I'm fine."

"Good. What are you doing today?"

"I'm going to the house at the end of the street."

"Stay safe."

It was his own private Wilson. It also had a few other neat functions, like a heart rate monitor that told him when he was too excited, and reminders for when to eat and take a nap. Ben could even control certain functions in the house form the device. It had become his partner in crime. He had even given it a British woman's accent. He had an odd relationship with it in some sick yet acceptable way. Her name was Eve.

For this little chat, the watch had been programmed to say good morning between set hours when his heart rate elevated to a certain level, which usually meant after coffee.

Walking into the house, Ben set down the mug before heading off for a shower. He often found himself feeling guilty for how nice things were. Warm running water, power, and a lot of booze stashed away.

Ben's mind wandered as it often did toward thoughts of Sarah, filling his mind with memories of her under the sprinkling water of the shower. He wondered where she was, and if she was safe. Would she still love him when she got back? All the bullshit couples thought about when they were apart.

Something was bothering Ben, however. Time was moving forward and Sarah was not home yet. Over time, Ben had taken a few maps, and with the help of some old college math textbooks he had found in storage, he had figured out how long it would take for her to get back. It was one of the first things he had done when all communication with the outside world had been cut. The calculations had included stops, incidents, and weather. The time was getting close. He had predicted it would take her roughly a year if she didn't travel by vehicle.

He figured vehicles were probably off the table, as he hadn't heard more than a handful over the year. After watching one too many zombie movies, he wasn't going to poke around to find out.

Ben, again following his daily routine, walked over to his map and calendar and marked off another day. Tomorrow would be in the red zone, as he called it. He projected she would be close soon. Thoughts of leaving out signs crossed his mind, letting Sarah know he was in fact there. He would figure that piece out soon.

Today marked eleven months and fifteen days since the world as he knew it had ended. She had been gone several months prior to that point, and he had counted every day since the last full call he had received from her—shortly after the evacuations had started—toward the one-year mark. The message he had received a few months ago justified everything he was doing.

Showered and shaved, Ben went into the master bedroom, laying out his equipment for the day.. It included protective clothing, combat boots, and general items he may need in case of an emergency, including some type of weapon. He kept the good stuff in his room.

Ben looked at himself in the mirror. His face was attractive, strong and kempt. The exercise and healthy living, for the most part, had treated him well over the past year. The light scar above his right eye stood out on an otherwise blank canvas. He lightly combed his hair back, pulling it behind his ears. While he usually kept it trimmed, he had decided to let it grow out last fall. Years of healthy living had covered up the tough years of his often times troubled youth.

The light smell of the approaching fall hung in the air, accompanied by the scent of a burning vanilla candle. Sarah was one of those candle types. She had candles for every season and occasion, from date night to afternoon cocktails with friends, which always ended up being experienced through smell.

While Ben had power, it wasn't enough to run the house fully. He could run the AC, but to the detriment of other systems, so he ran it sparingly. As was the case most days, he opened the windows, ran the fans, and let Mother Nature do all the work as he prepared to leave.

Even though Ben knew the neighborhood was empty, he was always cautious when leaving the main property. As he did on these occasions, Ben talked through his routine.

"Jeans, yup. Long sleeve undershirt, yup. Boots, ahh . . . these will do for today," Ben said, pulling out the new tan combat boots—which just happened to be a perfect fit—that he had found in the admiral's house next door. It also happened to be where he had acquired a semiautomatic M4 assault rifle with all the fixings, a lightweight plate carrier to attach things on, and his favorite scavenged item so far: one of those big ass Rambo-looking knives.

The pistol he carried around was actually his, and also a rather nice hunting rifle, but on the tactical side of things, his defense was far inferior to that of his neighbor's.

The only thing better, in his opinion, was the stockpile of steroids he had found in Jake's house, the ex-football player. Ben had decided to spend some time bulking up, and after studying the books he had also found stashed, had decided to fill his body with the muscle-building chemicals.

He had always thought those supplements were supposed to make you go all crazy. Nothing could have been further from the truth. When taken properly, and the proper type, he felt rejuvenated. Altogether, Ben had packed on fifteen pounds of muscle, stopping a few months back as the book recommended. Plus, he was sure their shelf life would soon run out, and didn't want to risk it.

He often dreamed of Sarah blushing when she saw him again.

After a few more minutes of prep, Ben headed downstairs, grabbing the keys to his prior-athlete neighbor's Toyota Tacoma. He had pulled it into his garage as one of a handful of exit routes in case his Tesla couldn't make it.

The Toyota was a hybrid and didn't care if it drank gas or electricity, but the fuel was still usable, and he had a stock of stabilizer he had gathered from the other boat owners. By his measure, including the latest developments in gas, the fuel would last roughly two to three years, maybe a little longer if he could manage it.

Over the past five years, almost half the cars on the road were electric. That, however, created a whole other level of shit-stirring problems. While fuel would last for years if stored properly, getting a stable current of electricity outside of his domain was going to be an issue. Either way, it was time for Ben to leave his personal paradise and go through the last house in the neighborhood.

Author Bios

Hunter Blain

My name is Hunter, and I'm a wordaholic. I'm also about to break the fourth wall...of your mindhole. Because there is a true story behind this...well...story.

It begins with two best friends who grew up together, breaking rules and raising hell as they shaped each other's personalities into the shameless assholes they are today. Well, at least for one of them, but I'll get to that in a moment. These two boys—let's call them Hunter and John—were all but inseparable. John excelled at creating music powerful enough to make angels weep and being the funniest asshole in Texas while Hunter dabbled—poorly, I might add—in his humble writings. Because they were self-declared brothers from other mothers, John respected Hunter's humble writings as much as I—I mean Hunter (stupid third person perspective)—respected John's musical magic. John's tunes could have changed the world, one day...

One fine day, after reading one of Hunter's horrifically detailed short stories about a serial killer, John asked Hunter to write a story about him.

"Hell yeah, dude! What do you want to be?" Hunter asked, brimming with honor and biting back a very manly squee.

"A vampire," John responded with a mischievous gleam in his eye. "But not one of those sparkly ones. A true bad ass!"

"Done!" Hunter crowed with a smile and an accompanying high five.

"No, dude. Promise. Promise you'll write and finish a book about me. You are the most prolific writer of our generation!" John said.

(Something like that. I might be paraphrasing a little, but you get the gist of it). "I would consider it an honor to live on for eternity with your words as my life's blood."

Hunter agreed, never to realize the weight of that promise until one Sunday morning when John's mother called, crying incoherently. John…had died.

Hunter was left in a cold world without his best friend and doppelgänger. Hunter still thinks about that moment to this day. How the morning light crept through the bedroom window while Hunter stared at the ceiling, noticing how the popcorn texture created cruel, jagged shadows. How everything started to blur as his chest was crushed beneath the weight of what he was hearing, each word stacking heavily upon the other until only fitful, ragged gasps of air could escape his throat. Only fiery tears existed, especially after the horrific realization that Hunter now had to make some of the hardest phone calls of his life to the circle of friends who orbited around John's solar pull.

Their star was no more, leaving their universe a colder and darker place.

John not only left Hunter, but a friend named Valenta as well. There was also Nathanial and Depweg. The friends were each stricken numb with the loss of such a beloved flare of life. But…

When the three found out that Hunter was keeping his promise to write the greatest story ever told—starring their dear friend, John—they demanded to be a part of the adventure. Each of them immediately knew what type of supernatural character they wanted to play in this urban fantasy eulogy. It would be a funeral pyre of words, and their fictional personas would be John's pallbearers.

So please, if you read the Preternatural Chronicles, feel free to laugh. Laugh at the situations John is placed in and his dickish dialogue to those around him, because John is 100% in this story without alteration (albeit he is a vampire). Laugh and let his memory live on inside the theater of your mind. Like he does in ours.

Thank you, sincerely, from the bottom of my beating heart, for giving my best friend the chance to live again. You are part of this magical ritual, and that would make him the happiest man in the... well, wherever the hell he is.

Deliverance: Book 0.5 of the Preternatural Chronicles
Facebook—Hunter Blain Author
www.HunterBlain.com

Justin S. Leslie

Justin is a retired, highly decorated army major who completed several tours in Afghanistan. He started writing after his misadventures landed him back in the real world and everyday life. This outlet has allowed Justin to indulge in often-needed escapes from the rat race.

Justin has focused on building his own magical worlds to share with readers, as well as enjoying ones created by fellow authors. He is in fact a huge book nerd…

He also holds an MBA from the University of Maryland with a Bachelors from Maryville College, and currently runs a national sales program for one of those big mega companies.

When he isn't writing, playing music or spending time with his wife and two boys, he can be found in his Doctors Inlet home, immersed in the latest urban fantasy, or a well-made old fashioned. His inspiration has come from all the other authors in the genre who've helped him through endless tough hours needing to take a break.

Note from author: Yes, I didn't write all that cheesy stuff above… maybe just some of it.

I hope everyone enjoys this collection of short stories. These are some great authors and its been an honor to get to know them.

To all my brothers and sisters in the armed forces. Cheers, and may the wind be forever at your back. To those we've lost along the way you will be forever missed.

"Halfway down the trail to Hell in a shady meadow green,"

www.justinleslie.com
Facebook—Justin Leslie
Buy Max Abaddon and the Will Book 1
Buy Max Abaddon and the Purity Law Book 2

Devin Hanson

Devin Hanson (1983–present) was born in Beaverton, Oregon. After a childhood spent programming computers and playing Dungeons and Dragons, Devin's career took a random turn to counseling.

It was during his years as a counselor that he developed his insight into the human condition and renewed his interest in writing. Currently, Devin works as a web developer, spending his free time creating tales of fantasy and science fiction. Devin has recently escaped Los Angeles and has moved down to San Diego.

www.devinhanson.com
Facebook—Devin Hanson
Buy The Halfblood's Hoard (Halfblood Legacy Book 1)

CT PHIPPS

C.T Phipps is a lifelong student of horror, science fiction, and fantasy. An avid tabletop gamer, he discovered this passion led him to write and turned him into a lifelong geek. He is a regular blogger on "The United Federation of Charles"

unitedfederationofcharles.blogspot.com

He's the author of *Agent G, Cthulhu Armageddon, Lucifer's Star, Straight Outta Fangton,* and *The Supervillainy Saga.*

ctphipps.wordpress.com
Facebook—CT Phipps
Buy Straight *Outta Fangton: A Comedic Vampire Story*